WhenTinkerMetBell

ALETHEA KONTIS

Sugar Skull Books LLC

When Tinker Met Bell

A Nocturne Falls Universe Story

A NOTE FROM KRISTEN PAINTER

Dear Reader,

Nocturne Falls has become a magical place for so many people, myself included. Over and over I've heard from you that it's a town you'd love to visit and even live in! I can tell you that writing the books is just as much fun for me.

With your enthusiasm for the series in mind – and your many requests for more books – the Nocturne Falls Universe was born. It's a project near and dear to my heart, and one I am very excited about.

I hope these new, guest-authored books will entertain and delight you. And best of all, I hope they allow you to discover some great new authors! (And if you like this book, be sure to check out the rest of the Nocturne Falls Universe offerings.)

For more information about the Nocturne Falls Universe, visit http://kristenpainter.com/sugar-skull-books/

In the meantime, happy reading!

~ Kristen Painter

∾

For Margo
On stage and off — NTs forever

∾

It was a beautiful day in Nocturne Falls.

According to every weather app on every smart phone in the world, the forecast for all of Georgia was blistering sun with a hundred percent chance of storms. Translation: Hot and humid with a side of sticky gross—not even remotely winterlike.

But Bellamy Merriweather Larousse woke up this morning and *chose* to have a beautiful day, and so it was.

"What can I get you, Mr. Hardwin?" she chirped brightly.

"One iced Draculatté, please, Bellamy. To go." Nick Hardwin pulled a few napkins from the dispenser beside the flyers for the Frozen in Fear Festival. "This heat is intense," he said, patting the damp hair at the nape of his neck. He raised a scarred eyebrow at the flyers. "Fear might show up, but I don't think Frozen got the memo about this month's shindig."

Bellamy's heart went out to the man, one of The Hallowed Bean's regulars. While most customers this time of day were stopping in to the coffee shop on their way home from the office, Bellamy knew Mr. Hardwin would be working deep into the night, either at Insomnia or the gargoyle fountain.

"How about I blend this for you?" Bellamy asked. "It'll taste like a coffee snow cone."

Mr. Hardwin's smile mirrored Bellamy's own. "That sounds amazing. Make it an extra-large. *Two* extra larges. I'll drop one by the jewelry shop. Willa will love it."

"Comin' right up!" Bellamy punched the sale into the register. It was sweet of him to be so considerate of his lady-love. In the back of her mind, Bellamy wished that someday someone would love her as much as Nick Hardwin loved Willa Iscove. But that was someday. Right now she was surrounded by some of the best friends in the world and, for Bellamy, that kind of love was enough.

Bellamy did a twirl as she set about concocting Mr. Hardwin's order. There was just something magical about the cheerful whirring of the blender on a hot day and Bellamy chose to honor that. She placed two drops of raspberry sauce inside each of the clear plastic cups and let them artfully slide down like drops of blood. Then she poured in the coffee blend, topping it off with a bit of whipped cream and dark chocolate drizzle. With a flick of her wrist, she secured the covers of both cups and slid them over to Mr. Hardwin with two giant wrapped straws.

"May you think only cold thoughts," she whispered to him conspiratorially.

"I'm sure I will if you say so," he said. "Thank you, Bellamy. You're one of the good fae."

Mr. Hardwin knew more than a few fae, both good and bad, so Bellamy took his compliment to heart. Especially since her particular brand of faeness wasn't the usual sort one generally found in Nocturne Falls. Bellamy had been born with wings, a throwback to the windkin on her mother's side, a fae bloodline that originated in another world entirely separate from this one.

They were beautiful wings, large enough to lift Bellamy in the air and carry her for miles, but she was as much at the mercy of the currents as any other bird or butterfly. She had no power over air, or stone, or fire, or metal. She could barely walk and chew gum at the same time. But she had fairy dust, shed from her wings. With it, she could manifest certain magic for short periods of time.

And she could work a cappuccino machine like nobody's business.

Mr. Hardwin took the drinks and stuffed a few dollars into the jack-o-lantern tip jar. An electronic werewolf howled as he walked out the front door. Sometimes that chime got so annoying that Bellamy disabled it. But not today. Because today was a beautiful day.

"Ahem."

Bellamy leaned back to see the person hidden by the giant espresso machine. She spotted the wild emerald green hair before the rest of him came into view. Today was getting better and better!

"Hey, Tinker. What's up?"

A visit from Tinker outside school always cheered Bellamy up. He was her oldest and best guy-friend—actual "bestest" best friend status was reserved for Kai Xanthopoulos, daughter of the managers over at Mummy's Diner.

Tinker had a gangly build and bumpy, sallow green skin, which looked extra sickly today. Probably because of the heat —it really did have no business being this hot so close to winter break. Some of Tinker's bumps came from his warty goblin heritage, but some were just acne. A temporary problem, but Tinker was so hard on himself about the way he looked.

Bellamy was always reminding Tinker that outward

appearance was an ever-changing thing. She had known him long before those awkward teenage years, when they were mischievous children of the same height playing pranks on their teachers. But now he towered over her just like he towered over everyone. The more he grew, the more he slouched. Bellamy wished he had the confidence to stand tall. But whatever part of his appearance aged back to "normal" over time, there would be no changing his height.

Tinker adjusted his glasses as his green eyes looked up at the decorated menu board. "I'll have what he had," he said, thumbing over his shoulder after Mr. Hardwin. "But without the hit of fairy dust."

Happily, Tinker was not so tall that Bellamy couldn't still grab him by the collar and yank his face down to hers. "Ranulf Tinkerton, what is *wrong* with you? Are you tryin' to get me fired?"

"I know that flick of the wrist all too well, Miss Larousse," he countered in a dramatic whisper. "You can't fool me."

He was right, of course. Bellamy always kept a small supply of fairy dust in the bracelet on her left wrist. "So I added some extra-frostiness to his beverage. So what? The poor man is dyin' in this heat. No harm done."

"The poor man?" Green eyebrows arched above Tinker's glasses. "You make him sound like some withered old thing. Nick Hardwin could bench press a school bus."

Bellamy released Tinker's shirt. She smoothed it back down as she narrowed her eyes at him, carefully touching only the fabric and not his skin. "You're just jealous."

Tinker stood still as a gargoyle himself while she straightened his collar. "Darn tootin'. I can sprain a wrist picking up a pipette. As you well know."

Bellamy almost laughed at that, but she stopped herself just in time. On the one wing, she had always loved Tinker's self-deprecating humor. On the other, she wished he at least thought as highly of himself as she did. It was true: Tinker *had* sprained his wrist in Chemistry class last year. He'd lifted that pipette right before slipping in a puddle of water some of the were-jocks had been splashing at each other and neglected to clean up.

"I blame that on the evils of dihydrogen monoxide," Bellamy said with a smile, referring to one of Tinker's particular nerdy science jokes. People often assumed that Bellamy's constantly cheerful demeanor and thick southern accent meant that she was stupid. Tinker had never treated her that way, and she respected him for that.

And the dihydrogen monoxide—water—*had* been evil...as had the thoughtlessness of others. That thoughtlessness seemed to occur around Tinker more than most. Especially at school. Sometimes, it was because he was just so dang smart. Sometimes, it was just because he was a goblin.

Tinker put a hand over his heart dramatically. "Dihydrogen monoxide! My nemesis! Say, now...I don't suppose you could sprinkle a little extra something on my drink that would turn me into a super strong chick magnet?"

Bellamy made a face at him. "All you need, mister, is little bit of self-confidence and some decent luck. Like I keep tellin' you." She lifted her left hand in the air and mimed poking him in the nose for good measure, without actually touching him.

Some of the dust must have escaped her bracelet, because Tinker threw his head back and violently sneezed into the handkerchief he'd pulled from his pocket. The sheer volume of the blast almost shook the windows. He held up a hand to the customers sitting at tables, including the one where Hubble, Sam, and Natalie stared at Tinker with more interest than usual. "Allergies," he explained to the cafe.

"Bless you," Bellamy said when Tinker turned back to the

counter. She followed up with a whispered, "Sorry. Are you all right?"

Tinker nodded. He wiped his watering eyes and blew his nose again.

Bellamy felt terrible. She knew better than to get any of her fairy dust on Tinker. Goblins were allergic to fairies. Miraculously, that hadn't stopped Tinker and Bell from being friends all this time, a fact that brought her great joy. But she should have known better. She could talk to Tinker all day long, but she could never, ever touch him.

"I'll make you that drink. On the house. But your fellow adventurers have to pay," she added, glancing over to the table by the window.

"Noted," Tinker said with a sniffle.

Bellamy plucked a clear plastic cup off the top of the stack. She wrote "Tinker" on the side and drew a smiley-faced butterfly before scooping out the ice for his drink. Out of the corner of her eye she spotted him stuffing the tip jar with cash he could ill afford. She scowled, but she knew arguing with him would be futile. She finished making his frozen Draculatté quickly and carefully, filling it with only good wishes and none of her tainted faeness.

Tinker might have been an awkward misfit from a race of misfits, but he had a good head, and a great heart. He deserved so much happiness...far more happiness than he received at school, at any rate. Tinker was one of the good ones. Funny how few of the other students at Harmswood managed to see that. If she could have used her fairy dust to change things, she would have.

Every morning, Bellamy tidied up the excess dust from her wings, leaving trails of sparkling rainbow magic all over the bathroom. She always made sure to save a little bit for her friends...and her favorite customers.

Bellamy was the highest-tipped barista in the history of

The Hallowed Bean, thanks to the extra little pick-me-ups folks had come to expect from their orders. A dash of Bellamy's dust might manifest as a selfless act or a kind word in someone's day. Fairy dust could coax a few more miles out of a car low on gas, or burn a few more calories during a morning workout. The effect of the dust was always temporary, and it never caused harm to anyone...who wasn't a goblin. The smiles and friendships the dust evoked lasted far longer than the magic itself.

But the last thing Bellamy wanted to do was kill one of her best friends in the whole wide world. Or make him sick. Or whatever other horrible thing might happen if a goblin like Tinker ingested a double-shot of fairy dust. Neither of them wanted to find out.

"Hey, Bell," he said as she slid over the large cup of bleeding-raspberry-and-chocolate amazingness. "You going to the Midwinter Masquerade?"

"Of course!" she answered happily. She was more excited about the Midwinter Masquerade than she was about the Frozen in Fear Festival, winter break, and the possibility of cooler weather combined. "Kai and I are on the decoratin' committee. It's gonna be *amazeballs*. Just wait until you see everything. You will see, won't you? I mean, you're goin', right?"

"Um..." Tinker suddenly looked ill. Had she accidentally dosed him again? He fiddled with his straw wrapper. "Well...yeah."

Bellamy kept the pleasant smile plastered to her face, but based on his reaction, she worried that she'd said something wrong. Tinker rarely attended school events. Had she just forced him to go to the masquerade against his will? He had been the one to bring it up... "Wonderful!" she said. "It will be so much fun."

"Yeah," Tinker said again. He started to back away from

the counter, as if he couldn't get away from her fast enough. Maybe he was just really thirsty?

"Save me a dance?" she asked after him.

He gave a half-laugh. "Absolutely." And then he turned and hurried back to his table.

Bellamy turned away too, so that no one in the coffee shop could see her frown. Maybe Tinker already had plans to go with someone else? Natalie had been staring at him rather intently... Sufferin' coffee stains! If he did already have a date, then Bellamy never should have forced him to promise her a dance like that. She'd be livid if her date took off to dance with someone else in the middle of the evening. Okay...well, truthfully she *wouldn't*...but most girls would. Especially Natalie.

Not that Bellamy would even have a date in the first place. She was an odd fae who hung with the locals. She may have been a cheerleader, but she wasn't the kind of girl that the rich boarding school boys at Harmswood wanted to date. That was another reason Tinker was so easy for Bellamy to be around. He'd gotten into Harmswood on a scholarship—the first goblin student in Harmswood history. He appreciated the little things.

Maybe he'd been put off by her suggestion to dance? Bellamy couldn't touch Tinker outright, but a pair of gloves could solve that problem easily enough...

She balled her fists. She wished she could dose herself with dust, if only to prevent her from putting her foot in her big fat mouth again. *Oh, Bellamy, you ever-lovin' truffle. Let it go. It's Tinker. Tinker would never be mad at you!*

But there was a first time for everything...

Bellamy put a smile back on her face and turned back to the cafe. Tinker was engrossed in some serious conversation with his friends. It was too late now for her to take back whatever silly thing she had said that caused him to cut their conversation short and walk away. She made a mental note to ask him about this tomorrow in Physics. And possibly apologize. A lot. Whatever mess she'd stepped in, deep down she knew Tinker would forgive her. Because she loved that jolly green giant to the moon, and he loved her right back.

And because today was a beautiful day.

2

This day was seriously starting to suck.

Tinker plopped down in the cafe chair and banged his knee on the metal bar under the tiny table. His wince of pain was masked by Hubble's aggravated growl as his DM screen flopped onto the tabletop.

"Hey now!" Hubble snatched up the screen. He re-bent the creases of the modified folder so that it would continue to shield his pile of ragged-edged notebook papers from the rest of the table. "Watch it, Tinkerton. There is sensitive material back here."

"Deciphering launch codes again? I was only gone five minutes."

"Nah," said Natalie. "Sam's dwarf tripped on a lever that opened a secret door in the passageway, and now Dungeon Master Hubble is rolling to answer like fifty questions that determine just how screwed we are."

Sam leaned back in his chair and yawned at the ceiling. "Sorry, guys. What can I say? I'm a clumsy dwarf. I didn't realize this was going to take foreeeeeeveeeeeer."

There was a clatter of dice and Hubble giggled like a

comic book villain from behind the screen. "I hope you like orcs…"

"I skewer them with my massive longsword!" cried Natalie.

"Hold your horses, Leeroy Jenkins," Hubble muttered. "We're not ready for that yet."

Tinker could only assume that "we" referred to Hubble and his newly-formed legion of bloodthirsty orcs.

"Well, hurry up so I can roll for an orc-kebab." Natalie rubbed her hands together. "I'm still annoyed you cancelled our rehearsal for this, but I'm feeling lucky. And speaking of lucky"—she leaned over to Tinker and stage-whispered —"did you ask her?"

Sam picked his head back up to stare at his sister. "Subtle, Nat. Real subtle."

Natalie put a hand to her ear. "What's that, narcoleptic?" she said loudly. "I can't hear you. I think you're sleep-talking again."

"Jeez, Nat." Sam rubbed his eyes with the back of his hands. "I am exhausted, though. Maybe I'll get a coffee." He nodded to Tinker's drink. "That looks good. What's that?"

"It's a—"

"—something you won't be having, bro," Natalie finished. "The last time you drank coffee before the full moon, you were incapacitated for a week."

Sam stuck his tongue out at his little sister, but only because what she said was absolutely true. Sam was a were-sloth. On top of being constantly tired, during the full moon —and after caffeine crashes—Sam turned into a sweet, furry, immovable lump.

Sam and Natalie's family had recently moved to the Falls from some small town in northern Virginia where, in December of 2012, everyone had shifted into a were-being of their totem animal. Everyone, that is, except a select few…

including Natalie. Since she'd missed the magical boat, Natalie had become the one in charge of wrangling her wild were-family when they couldn't manage themselves. Which also qualified her to be one of the rare plain-old-human students at Harmswood.

Well, as plain-old as any girl could be in four-inch, knee-high platform pleather boots and black lipstick. She'd immediately teamed up with Hubble and his theatre troupe, and it felt like she'd always been part of the school. In only a few months, Natalie fit in better among the paranormals at Harmswood than Tinker had the entire time he'd been there.

"Go on," Tinker said to Sam. "I'm sure Bellamy would be happy to hook you up with a decaf."

"'Southern Bell' is always happy," said Natalie. She glanced at Hubble, his silver-gray head still bent over his dice as he scribbled calculations. She asked Tinker her question again, this time in an actual whisper. "So did you invite her to the masquerade or not?"

"Sort of," he said.

"Well, did she say yes?"

"Sort of," he said again.

Natalie sighed. "Tink, sweets, I'm dying over here. You're going to have to give me a little more to go on."

Tinker pinched the bridge of his nose and summoned all the patience he could muster. Natalie could be abrasive, but she was usually right. Especially when it came to Tinker and his complete lack of confidence around girls.

Scratch that, *girl*. One girl. Bellamy.

It had always been Bellamy.

He remembered the moment he'd first laid eyes on her, like a photograph frozen in his mind forever. She sat illuminated by the window of his fourth grade classroom. She'd been wearing a pink sundress, with those gigantic wings and that head full of bouncy golden ringlets. When she turned to him she'd given him that thousand-watt smile that shone like the sun, and the rest of the horrible world just melted away.

When most people laid eyes on Tinker—even back when he was a plump little greenling—they wrinkled their noses in confusion or disgust, as if he wore a sign that labeled him a slimy, sickly, bumpy, unwanted street rat. Paranormals and humans alike judged him and found him wanting before he ever spoke a word. Despite his scholarship, he'd had to work extra hard in every class and excel at every course of study before most of the teachers at Harmswood had taken him seriously.

But not Bellamy.

Bellamy believed the best of everyone until they proved her wrong, and even then she gave them a second chance. Years ago, that fairy girl had smiled at that goblin boy like she'd been waiting for him all morning and couldn't believe he'd finally arrived. It didn't matter that goblins were allergic to fairies. It didn't matter that goblins and fairies shouldn't be friends. Bellamy Larousse could have been a golem made out of napalm and cyanide and Tinker wouldn't have cared. He'd lost his heart that day. Lost and gone forever.

Snap.

Tinker focused on Natalie's fingers, mere inches from his face. "Earth to Tink. You still with us?"

"Sorry." He shook his head. "What?"

"What. Did. She. Say. Exactly?" Natalie said in her best William Shatner imitation.

"She's on the decorating committee with Kai," he answered. "She doesn't need anyone to escort her to the masquerade because she'll already be there when the doors open."

Natalie crossed her very long legs and folded her very long arms. Natalie didn't quite have Tinker's height, but she was definitely taller than Sam. Especially in those shoes.

"Yeah. Well, I can believe she said the first part, but I'm pretty sure you inferred the last bit."

"How in the world could you know that?"

"Because I'm way smarter than you or my brother will ever give me credit for. Now...what did Bellamy say, *exactly*?"

Tinker bowed his head and mumbled. "She asked if I would save her a dance, and I said I would."

Natalie pursed her lips. She stared at Tinker, then over at the counter where Bellamy was finishing up Sam's drink, and then back at Tinker. "I don't even know where to start. It's like you're *both* clueless."

Tinker sighed. "I know."

"Why don't you just...I don't know...walk up to her and tell her you love her?"

"Because he's already done that." Hubble peeked over the DM screen, squinting his piercing cobalt blue eyes. All the mine-dwelling kobolds possessed eyes that same bright color —it was only a little unnerving.

Glancing from Tinker to Natalie, Hubble went on. "Sixth grade. In which it was established that he loves her and she loves him." He recited the tidbit as if it were a historical fact from the textbook of Tinker's life.

Natalie raised an eyebrow. "So he should...ask her to marry him?"

"Eighth grade..." started Hubble.

Tinker groaned.

"...in which Tinker and Bellamy vowed that they would grow old together. And then there was this past summer..."

Tinker hung his head.

"...during which Tinker finally confessed to his goblin mentor that he was in love with a fairy."

"What did your mentor say?" Natalie asked incredulously. "Were you flogged or something for consorting with the enemy?"

"He didn't say anything," Tinker said. "He just changed the subject. So I didn't bring it up again."

"Oh, wow, that's harsh. But I guess it could have been worse." Natalie shook her head. "So...let me get this straight. Bellamy loves you and plans on spending the rest of her life with you, and you love her and have thought about pretty much nothing but her for years, but you guys aren't girlfriend and boyfriend?"

"Goblins and fairies can't be friends," said Tinker. "Never mind girlfriends or boyfriends."

"Star-crossed lovers," Hubble murmured over his dice.

Tinker scowled at his roommate and so-called best friend. Kobolds were similar to goblins in many ways; both races had reputations for being scavengers and hoarders. But if Hubble wanted to kiss a fae woman's hand, he could do so without breaking into swollen lips and hives.

Natalie wasn't buying any of it. "But you managed to be friends with her anyway, despite that stupid rule."

Tinker could feel his cheeks burning. Thankfully, green-skinned goblins didn't blush. Much. "Yes. We're just friends. Really good friends. Even though we shouldn't be."

"More precisely," said Hubble, "the 'girlfriend' thing is the one question he's too chicken to ask her."

Natalie reached out and smacked Tinker on the back of the head. He saw it coming, but he knew he deserved it.

"Look, I'm just no good with this stuff."

"No good with girls?" Hubble huffed. "Yeah. It's obvious."

"No good with feelings," muttered Tinker. "It's not like I grew up with a family or anything. I was an orphan, abandoned as a baby on the streets, picked up and adopted by goblins. I have no clue how to express emotions like this."

"Oh, sweetie, I've got news for you," said Natalie. "People all over the world have no idea how to express themselves.

Even ones who did grow up in regular families. Isn't that right, Sam?"

Sam had returned to the table with not only a frosty beverage for himself but also ones for Natalie and Hubble as well. "Whatever she said, she's absolutely correct."

Tinker had to hand it to Sam. He was a good brother.

Natalie took a sip of the frozen chocolate and closed her eyes for a moment in bliss. "I was telling Tink that he's not the only kid without the ability to properly communicate his feelings."

"You mean about Bellamy?" Sam shrugged as he slid languidly down into his chair. "I told him to just kiss her."

Natalie raised her glass to Sam. "Brother, that may be the most intelligent thing I've ever heard you say."

"Granted, that might kill him. Or send him into anaphylactic shock." Hubble rolled the dice again. "The school nurse has a file on him thicker than the D&D *Player's Handbook*."

Tinker had fantasized about kissing Bellamy a million times, not that he'd ever admit it to his friends. Every time, he had died a happy man. She would leave flowers on his grave regularly, and pine over the loss of him for the rest of her days. But he would never take that risk in real life. Never. He could never do that to Bellamy.

Sam shrugged. "Take a Benadryl."

After another sip of her drink, Natalie reconsidered. "It's possible that she doesn't *want* your relationship to go beyond friendship. In which case, you should respect that…"

Tinker pointed at Natalie. "Exactly! Well said."

"…*after* you ask her the girlfriend question," Natalie finished.

"Or just kiss her," Sam said around his straw.

Tinker smirked. "I am not going to assault one of my best friends and ruin the rare and beautiful relationship we have."

This time, Sam, Natalie, and Hubble all threw up their

hands in unison. Hubble's DM screen flopped back down to the table.

"I'm seriously considering assaulting one of *my* best friends," Hubble said to Tinker as he repositioned the screen. "Right after I crush his tiny little band of misfit adventurers with this horde of zombie orcs."

"Can my half-elf roll to fire an arrow at them through the secret door because they're taking so long to get ready?" asked Tinker.

"Dude." Sam snorted. "They're *teenage girl* zombie orcs."

Natalie kicked her brother's chair. "Check yourself, fuzzbutt. I know where you sleep."

"Got it!" Hubble clapped his hands together and rubbed them sinisterly. "Gird your loins, gamers. You are so not ready for this." Adopting his most dramatic Dungeon Master voice, Hubble spoke. "*Seemingly out of nowhere, a legion of orcs begins to pour through the secret doorway...*"

The electronic werewolf howled as the front door opened.

Tinker and his tiny band of misfit adventurers all burst out laughing.

"Ranulf Tinkerton!" a raspy voice called out.

Tinker froze mid-laugh. He recognized that voice, though he hadn't expected to see its owner again until winter break. Slowly, he turned in his chair. "Retcher?"

Yes, his goblin mentor was really there inside the coffee shop. Three more of the Lost Boys stood with him: Snot and the twins, Fork and Willie. How had they found him here, in the Bean? And what on earth were they doing in Nocturne Falls in the first place? Goblins weren't allowed to leave Goblin City, unless they had special dispensation from the Goblin King. Like the one Tinker had for his schooling, or the one Retcher possessed for gathering other Lost Boys and adding them to the tribe.

Retcher had rescued baby Tinker from the streets of Nowhere Special and welcomed him into the goblin fold. He had been the one to urge Tinker to go away to Harmswood. What on earth was he doing here?

After a few heartbeats, Tinker focused on what tiny, wide-eyed Snot carried in his oversized green hands.

No.

No, no, no, no, *no.*

No way.

This was not happening. Not today. Not ever. Not *here.* Not in front of...

"What is that thing?" he heard Natalie whisper.

"That thing" was an enormous, gaudy, borderline-lethal construction of tin garbage, an eyesore reserved for only one honor.

"It's a ceremonial headdress, given to the heir to the throne of the Goblin King," Tinker said softly. *But that's not me*, he screamed inside his brain. *This is not supposed to happen to me.*

"Holy—" Hubble clamped his own hand over his mouth before a curse escaped his lips. Sam let out a low whistle. Natalie pulled her phone out of her pocket and hit record.

Tinker scanned the coffee shop. Everyone was staring at him now. Including Bellamy.

Retcher stood as tall as his crooked frame allowed. His stringy black hair fell into his eyes, covering almost all of his face except his bulbous, warty nose. The twins flanked him proudly. Snot, predictably, sniffled. Unable to move his hands without dropping the headdress, he casually wiped his nose on the pillow where it sat.

"Ranulf Tinkerton," Retcher announced. "We bestow upon you the Mantle of Majesty."

The monstrosity should have been called the Mantle of Misfortune. Bits had been added to the headdress over the years: a spoon here, a button there, a bottle cap or two, all nestled among dozens of coin-sized pieces of hammered tin. It did not sparkle in the light like dwarven silver might have, nor did the pieces tinkle magically as Retcher moved to place it over Tinker's head and shoulders. Instead, it clattered.

"Henceforth, you will be known as the Goblin Prince, heir apparent to the throne of the Goblin King."

Tinker opened his mouth and then closed it again. He wasn't sure what to say. If anything. It wasn't like he'd ever rehearsed this ceremony, because *it wasn't supposed to happen to him*.

The headdress smelled like iron and old feet. It had knocked Tinker's glasses off kilter, so he shifted it enough to straighten them. Several bits of tin fell to the floor.

Hubble—dramatic Hubble, go-bold kobold and best friend a guy could ever have—stood on top of his chair, maximizing his height. He threw his gray arms wide and, in his best Dungeon Master voice, announced to the coffee shop, "Welcome to Nocturne Falls, everyone!"

At that, the confused occupants of The Hallowed Bean began to applaud and cheer, Sam and Natalie loudest of all. Thanks to Hubble's declaration, all the tourists in the Bean would now just write this off as one more impromptu performance, staged for their benefit. Out of the corner of his eye, Tinker saw Bellamy clapping too, her rainbow-streaked curls bouncing cheerfully. The smile plastered to her face was both sweet and mystified.

Tinker closed his eyes and wished with all his might that the earth would open up and swallow him and the Malevolent Mantle *right now*.

Oh, yeah. It was official.

Worst. Day. Ever.

3

Bellamy was up so early the next morning that she bumped into Asher at the bottom of the stairway on her way to the Harmswood dining hall. Asher was always in a hurry, rushing off to one place or another. Literally running into her older brother was the only way she saw him these days.

He was dressed in his Nocturne Falls tour guide uniform: pumpkin-orange polo and black slacks. Like most fae, Asher didn't have wings, just long, pointed ears and those trade-mark multicolor-blue eyes. Bellamy envied her brother's ability to purchase a shirt off the rack without having to modify it into a halter top. Wings were wonderful things, except when it came to clothing.

"Heya, Bell." He sounded in desperate need of a coffee.

"Mornin', Ash," she replied brightly.

"I heard your puppy got crowned king last night at the Bean. Is that true?"

Bellamy's light dimmed a bit, and she took back any pity she'd felt for her brother a moment ago. "Don't be rude. Tinker is not a dog. Least of all mine."

"I beg to differ, little sis. That poor goblin boy's been

wrapped around your little finger for years. If you said 'jump,' Tinker would ask how high."

"He would not," Bellamy said defiantly. Tinker would never ask such a ridiculous question. He'd just jump, because he trusted her. That's what friends did.

"Right. You keep telling yourself that."

"Why are you dressed for work? Shouldn't you be headed to class? I assume you have midterms, just like the rest of us."

"Got permission from the Head Witch to be excused today," he said. "She's calling it 'independent work-study.' This warm weather is bringing the tourists in droves. Retailers across town are already running out of inventory. And what with winter break right around the corner... If we don't hurry up and have a cold snap, Parks and Rec is going to need to hire more guides. Which reminds me—will your cheer squad be needing the pumpkinmobile anytime soon?"

As much as Asher teased Bellamy, her generous older brother did let her drive his official Nocturne Falls Parks and Recreation golf cart whenever she wanted. It looked like an enormous jack o'lantern, complete with lights and themed music, and she adored it. "This festival doesn't come with a parade. As for the masquerade, Kai and I lined up Ace and his gargoyle buddies to help us with the big stuff. We should manage just fine, thanks."

"Good. Between work and school, I suspect I won't be around much. And hey, if I somehow miss the masquerade, give Merri my best, will you?"

She was all ready to scold Asher about missing the ball she'd worked so hard on, and then his words sunk in.

"Merri's comin'?" Bellamy was torn between joy and panic. All Harmswood alumni were invited to participate in major school events. Few ever returned to do so. But Merri-aurum Grandiflora, oldest of the Larousse children, had always loved the Midwinter Masquerade. She did her best to attend whenever she could. And whenever she did, her penchant for matchmaking usually resulted in chaos.

Asher wrinkled his nose. "Oops. That might have been a secret. When she shows, try to act surprised, willya?"

Bellamy should have no trouble with that. "Will do," she said. "Good luck herding the tourists. I wish you lots of generous tips." She kissed her brother on the cheek and sent him on his way.

When she opened the doors to the dining hall, her eyes widened in shock. This hour of the morning on a normal day, the only ones in the dining hall were the early risers, the test-crammers, and whatever sports team had drill runs at the crack of dawn. Today, however, it looked like every boarding student in Harmswood had risen with the sun and come down for breakfast. The locals too: Kai caught Bellamy's eye and waved her over to the table where she and Finn and Owen were sitting.

"What in the world is goin' on? Thank you, Finn." Bellamy graciously took the stool Kai's boyfriend offered her. Chairs were not made for people with wings.

Maya Cordova—who was never up at this hour, never mind out of her house and already at school—slid a tray filled with coffee and pastries into the middle of the table. "Natalie's video went viral on the Harmswood intranet last night. We're all eagerly awaiting the appearance of our newly-crowned royalty."

Bellamy stood and immediately began fixing all her friends' coffees to their specifications, as if it was something she did all the time…because it was. It wasn't an inconvenience—Bellamy enjoyed doing things at which she excelled. Cream and sugar for Kai, mostly cream for Owen, a dash of sugar for Finn. Maya took hers black, but Bellamy gave her a healthy pinch of fairy dust to help make her morning a little less difficult. As she handed each cup to her friends, she watched them all take satisfied sips.

"Your coffee's always the best, Bell," Maya said with her eyes closed.

"Thanks, sweetie." Bellamy inhaled the rich aroma of the coffee in her own cup. Not quite the quality of the Bean, but still decent. "He's going to hate this, you know."

"Who, Tinker?" asked Finn.

"He's not one for attention," said Bellamy. "He prefers to fly under the radar."

"Why is that?" Owen asked in that lovely, slow English accent, almost as if he cared.

Finn and Owen, a wolf-shifter and cat-shifter respectively, had only just started school at Harmswood. Both were impossibly handsome, and both were insanely in love with Kai. But while Kai had chosen to give her heart to Finn, Owen still remained glued to her side.

Some girls had all the luck. Boys only flirted with Bellamy if they wanted fairy dust. Or free coffee.

"Historically, the only time the kids at this school have noticed Tinker is to make fun of him," Kai explained to her beaus.

Until that moment, the potential for mischief hadn't even occurred to Bellamy. "If these people are all waitin' around to make Tinker the butt of some awful joke, I swear I'll...I'll..." Honestly, she had no idea what she would do.

She felt a hand touch her arm: Maya. "Have faith, chica. If these fools act up, I'll curse the lot of them. And you know how we feel about cursing at this table."

"You wouldn't dare do such a thing," said Kai. "If you cursed anyone, the local coven would strip your powers faster than you could say 'boo.'"

"I'd do it for Bellamy," Maya said without pause. "And so would you. Because she's family."

Bellamy had a huge family—including a dozen brothers and sisters—but Maya's words still touched her. Her little circle of friends at Harmswood were the family Bellamy had chosen, and therefore very close to her heart. Maya wasn't one for overt displays of affection, especially this early in the morning, but Bellamy gave her a quick hug anyway.

"While I appreciate y'all offerin' to perform dastardly deeds on my behalf, I sincerely hope that won't be necessary."

"We're about to find out," said Finn. As one, they all turned their heads to the doors of the main entrance.

Tinker had just walked through them.

He stared apprehensively at the sea of faces that greeted him. They all stared back. Hubble Hobson snuck out from behind Tinker's looming form and stood proudly before his best friend.

"Harmswood, your prince has arrived!" Hubble's voice echoed across the entire dining hall.

There was a moment of silence, and then…cheers. Every sports team, every cheerleader, every member of a band or a club whistled and cried out for Tinker. The popular witches resignedly gave golf claps. Even the teachers applauded. It was like nothing Bellamy had ever seen before.

Tinker stood tall and, in a most un-Tinker-like manner, threw his arms up in a triumphant vee. Kids from all over the dining hall began to approach Tinker to shake his hand or pat him on the back.

"Is that what all the fuss was about?" Owen turned back to the table with a yawn. "I think your boy's going to be just fine."

"He's not mine," Bellamy muttered instinctively.

"Looks like he belongs to everyone at Harmswood today," said Maya. "Jealous much?"

Bellamy bit into a blueberry muffin. "Drink your coffee and stop bein' ridiculous."

"Come on, Bell." Kai chose the orange date scone and split it with Finn. "You've been Tinker's sun and moon and starlit sky since the day he got to this school. Having to share him with the world isn't going to bother you at all?"

Bellamy shrugged. "If he's happy, I'm happy."

Maya smirked. "That is such a Bellamy answer."

"You're welcome very much." Bellamy smirked right back. "Besides, no matter what happened last night, he's still my Physics lab partner. No giant crown is gonna take that away. Oh! That reminds me." She reached inside the magic pocket her mother had sewn into all her dresses and extracted the four pieces of hammered tin she'd rescued from the floor of the cafe during clean up. "These fell off his ceremonial thingamabob last night."

The four bits looked sort of like nickels that had been flattened with a ball-peen hammer. They were all a bit form-less, though one of them was vaguely heart-shaped. Each had a hole at one end where, presumably, they had been fastened onto the headdress. All of the holes had been ripped through.

"I was hopin' you might see what you could do to fix them," she said to Kai. Kai Xanthopulos was a Greek Fury. In addition to telepathy (which Kai found easier with animal-shifters) and vengeance (which she'd only used once), one of Kai's paranormal attributes was the ability to conduct massive amounts of heat.

Kai picked up the heart-shaped sliver of tin and examined it. "I haven't tried metalworking yet," she admitted, "but these seem light enough…hold on." She pinched the torn side of the hole between her thumb and forefinger, held it for a moment, and then rubbed back and forth quickly.

"There," she said with a smile. She held up the now-solid piece, one end still slightly orange from heat, and blew on it. She dropped it in Bellamy's hand before going to work on the other three. It was still warm.

"Thanks," she said to Kai. "I'm sure he'll appreciate it." Something as historical and significant as the Mantle that marked a boy Heir to the Goblin Throne should be kept as intact as possible. Which she said to Tinker, in so many words, when he plopped down on the stool beside her in the Physics lab later that afternoon. She waited for him to thank her profusely and smile at her with great enthusiasm.

Instead he said, "Just throw them away."

"I'm sorry?" Bellamy asked over her outstretched hand. She couldn't have heard him correctly.

"Trust me," said Tinker. "That thing's a big enough hunk of junk already. No one even noticed they were gone."

Bellamy slipped the metal bits back into her secret pocket. *She* had noticed. But Bellamy often noticed little things that didn't matter to other people. Clouds that looked like dragons. Rain, drawing its path down a window pane. The way snow lingered in the air instead of falling straight to the ground.

A lanky goblin boy who could solve algebraic calculations without even looking at his paper.

Bellamy had always been drawn to people and things that were otherwise out-of-the-ordinary. She supposed it was because she knew what it was like to be treated as "different." Kai—Bellamy's first and best friend—had been the one to step up and intercede when Bellamy was but a tiny fairy girl and all the other kids wanted to touch her, or pull at her golden hair, or rub up against her wings for "lucky dust." They told her she was "just like a doll." Her schoolmates were too young to realize that they were treating her like a thing instead of a person.

But Kai had put a stop to all that. She had forced the other children to introduce themselves to Bellamy properly. Taught them manners. Taught them to *ask* Bellamy for fairy dust instead of trying to just take it themselves. One of the reasons Bellamy had joined the cheer squad—apart from the singular opportunity to encourage folks to openly share their love for something—was so that Kai and Maya didn't have to be her bodyguards all the time. Once the squad got to know her, they—and whatever team they were cheering for—often acted as Bellamy's protection from outsiders.

Bellamy took it upon herself to dole out hugs and happiness. People were bound to find excuses to touch her—being in control of the situation seemed the best solution and put everyone at ease.

Still, Bellamy had wished many times to be naturally grotesque in appearance. To be someone that no one wanted to touch. She had been wishing that very thing while staring out the window in class one day, when the teacher had suddenly announced a new student.

When Bellamy first laid eyes on Tinker, she thought he was the most amazingly wonderful thing she'd ever seen in her life. It was as if fate had stepped through that door and given her the answer to her prayers.

And Tinker seemed to like her, too—genuinely like her as a person, not just a fairy. He wasn't even *supposed* to like her as a fairy. And he *couldn't* touch her, even if he wanted to. If he touched her, his goblin skin would break out in a rash. If he got too close, her dust would trigger a sneezing fit. They'd become friends not because of her magical fairy powers, but in spite of them.

Their friendship was everything Bellamy ever wanted.

Bellamy stared at Tinker while he extracted his Physics book from his bag. She examined the curve of his neck. The cluster of warts behind his large ear. His shaggy dark green hair, short at the nape but long enough in the front to fall dashingly over his eyes.

She wished that she could give him a giant hug without sending him to the nurse.

Had she taken their special bond for granted all these years? Tinker was a wonderful person. He *deserved* to be adored by everyone. But Maya had been right. This sudden popularity of his did bother Bellamy, and she had no idea why.

"I'm a horrible friend," she said quietly, as Professor Hagar began his lecture on reflection and refraction.

"Yes, I've always thought that about you," Tinker whispered back. Then he gave her that smirk—the one that meant he thought she was being ridiculous.

Professor Hagar paused to give Bellamy and Tinker a different sort of smirk. They both straightened in their seats and pretended to give him their full attention.

I didn't even ask how you are today, Bellamy wrote in her notebook. *Are you overflowing with happiness about your wonderful new position?* She slid the book over to where Tinker could see it.

After a cursory glance, he quickly wrote, *No.* His eyes stayed glued to Professor Hagar.

Bellamy didn't have to write anything after that. She only had to stare at Tinker long enough for him to see the expression on her face. He knew better than to leave her hanging with no information.

It wasn't supposed to be me, he added.

"I don't understand," Bellamy blurted aloud.

"Can I help you, Miss Larousse?" Professor Hagar asked.

Bellamy pointed to the acute angles her teacher had drawn on the board. "I'm sorry, sir. I didn't understand that last part of what you said." It was only sort of a lie.

As soon as Professor Hagar turned back to the board, Tinker grabbed the notebook and started scribbling furiously upon it. Bellamy tried to pay attention to the Physics lesson while Tinker wrote.

"Concave instead of convex," Bellamy repeated back to Professor Hagar. "Thank you, sir. I think I have it now."

Tinker followed up Bellamy's comment with a question of his own. "So would spells act the same way through those lenses as light does?"

Professor Hagar lit up. "That's a very good question, Mr. Tinkerton. In fact, that is the point of this lesson. As you'll see…"

Tinker winked at Bellamy and slid the notebook back over to her while Professor Hagar was distracted. He had written a lot.

The Goblin Prince is supposed to be a boy named Quin Merchero. Maybe something happened to him? I don't know. Retcher and his crew just gave me the Mantle and left. But they'll be back.

The Goblin King rules over the goblins. Protects them. He's in charge of finding new Lost Boys, adding them to the goblin horde, and stopping anyone who tries to steal them back. (No one ever has in my lifetime, but there are stories.) A prince doesn't need to be good at math or science. He doesn't get sent to school. It's not supposed to be me. Leaving Harmswood makes me the opposite of happy.

Bellamy read the note three times. Every time it ended with the same conclusion: the goblins were coming back to pull Tinker out of school. But when? And why did it suddenly feel like there was a night-hag sitting on her chest? Bellamy forced herself to take a deep breath and calmly wrote back.

You can't leave yet. You still owe me a dance.

Tinker gave a half-laugh at her note, and shook his head. *I'll do my best,* he wrote. To Professor Hagar, he asked, "Does that mean if a witch casts a spell through a magnifying glass, she could kill a person?"

On any other day, the class would have shifted and

groaned at Tinker's questions. Today, they all laughed and burst out with supporting comments.

"Don't let Heather find out about this," one student called out.

"I'd be more worried about Maya," called another.

"Forget Maya. Just think what Professor Blake could do to you!" This last comment triggered a shouted chorus of random nonsense spell words from the Harry Potter books.

"Now, now, everyone, calm down," said Professor Hagar.

Bellamy put her hand into the air. "Professor Hagar? May I please use the restroom?"

"Yes, Miss Larousse. Settle down, class. The short answer to Mr. Tinkerton's question is actually 'yes.' The longer answer depends on the exact spell, the curve of the lens, and specific physical principles…"

Bellamy eased out of the chaotic room and shut the door on Professor Hagar's sentence. She didn't need to go to the restroom. She wasn't sure exactly what she needed at the moment beyond getting out of that room and finding a place to breathe. Or scream.

Tinker was leaving Harmswood.

Not here. She couldn't scream here. Or outside. Someone would hear.

Her room. She could scream in her room. With everyone in class, no one would be around to worry about her. She would have plenty of time to compose herself before she saw her friends again. Before she saw Tinker again.

The stabbing pain in her chest made her wince. She launched into the air and sped off toward the girls' wing as fast as she could.

"No flying in the hallways, Miss Larousse," she heard some professor say, but she ignored it. If she didn't fly away right now, she might very well fall down dead instead. No one wanted that.

She burst through the door of her room, slammed it behind her, and then screamed as loud as she could. Louder than she'd ever screamed at a pep rally. She screamed until all the air in her lungs was gone. She took a deep breath and screamed again. Three times. Four. Finally exhausted, she sank down to the floor in a puff of rainbow-colored dust and wept.

The door clicked open and tiny feet slipped through. Lian Chong, her roommate. A flower fae.

"Bellamy?" Lian's voice was as dainty as her step.

"Shouldn't you be in class?" Bellamy hiccuped.

"I was," she said. "Professor Van Zant saw you in the hallway and was worried, so he sent me up here after you. Bellamy, sweetheart, whatever is the matter? This isn't like you."

"I know. I'm sorry." It was true. No one ever saw Bellamy Larousse cry, and Bellamy Larousse made sure of that. But Lian was the closest thing she had to a sister right now, so Bellamy told her the truth. "I just found out that Tinker's goin' to have to leave school and...I guess it just hit me rather hard."

"You *guess*? Honey, if you could see yourself right now..."

"...I'd give myself a hug and a cup of coffee?" Bellamy's laugh turned into a sob. "I can't even hug him goodbye! How fair is that?" Her eyes filled with so many tears that Lian's shape blurred before her. "And why am I actin' like a six-year-old? What is wrong with me?"

Lian slid to the floor beside Bellamy and handed her a tissue to dry her tears. "You're upset because he's one of your best friends and you love him," she said softly. "And because you never lose people."

Bellamy smiled, as if the act of doing so might automatically dry up the tears. It didn't. "How can I lose something I never had?" she asked her friend. "Everybody keeps referrin' to him as 'my' Tinker. But he's not 'my' anythin'. He doesn't belong to anyone but himself."

"Bellamy, Tinker has been yours since the moment he met you, and the only one who can't seem to see that is *you*." Lian gave an unfairylike snort. "Must be part of the whole 'love is blind' thing."

"Goblins and fairies can't be anythin' to each other," said Bellamy. "They can't even touch."

"Hearts don't have to touch to fall in love," said Lian.

Bellamy put a hand over her mouth in an attempt to cover the sob that broke out. Lian was right. Bellamy had *fallen in love* with her best friend. A goblin she shouldn't have been friends with in the first place. It had happened so gradually, over so many years, that she hadn't even realized.

But apparently everyone else had.

Young Bellamy had wished for someone who could be friends with her without wanting to touch her all the time, without her permission. When the universe had provided, she'd gone and fallen in love with him. And now he was leaving her forever.

"Here." Lian opened her arms wide. "You can't hug him, but you can hug me."

Bellamy threw herself into her friend's embrace and hugged her tightly—so tightly—as she cried her heart out all over again.

4

Tinker groaned as he turned on the water. Facing off against a gang of gargoyles had left him covered in dirt, with more than a few bruises. Apart from his injuries, nothing in his life seemed familiar anymore.

He'd been up before dawn again. This time he ended up running sprints with the track team. After that, he'd been roped into a makeshift flag football game: gargoyles versus weres. Tinker didn't have the first clue about the rules of football, but it seemed this morning's play was more about tackling the guy with the ball instead of actively trying to score any points. It was interesting: these same kids had beaten him up and ignored him for years, and now they invited him to join in. Turned out, *willingly* having the stuffing beat out of you was a lot more fun. Who knew?

Tinker smiled to himself and stepped in the shower. Tilted his face up to the spray. Let the warmth of the water sink into his bones.

Lately, all the stuff he normally did—reading, playing video games, inventing something new—just couldn't hold his attention. Ever since Retcher and his boys had crowned him with the Majestic Menace, there was this strange wild energy inside his belly. He wanted to jump out of his skin if he stood still too long.

Sam was familiar with this feeling. He said that most weres experienced something very similar every month around the full moon.

If Tinker didn't know better, he might have thought he was turning into a shifter himself. He was used to being weak, tired and anxious, with a constant headache. These past few days, he felt stronger. Centered. It was easier to move. To breathe. To think. Even his muscles ached in a good way.

Was it possible to catch health like catching a cold?

He also found it a lot easier to talk to people he didn't know very well. Which was a good thing, because suddenly everyone at Harmswood was talking to him like they'd known him forever. Most of them *had* known him for years, but he doubted any of them would have remembered his name before he'd been crowned heir to the goblin throne. Before Natalie's little video.

They all thought he was some grand prince now. No one seemed to care that he was destined to become King of Magpies and Stealer of Children. To the Harmswood populace, a throne was a throne, and a prince was a prince. Their friendships weren't real. They wouldn't last.

He didn't care.

Tinker was going to spend whatever time he had left at Harmswood as one of the most popular kids in school, and it felt good. It felt *great*! There was only one small flaw in this perfection, one tiny, shining string that pulled at his heart.

Bellamy.

Being around Bellamy was like torture. Every time he looked at her sweet face, he remembered everything he was about to lose. No more parades. No more coffee stops at the

Bean. No more D&D games with Hubble and the gang. No more preparing for college. No more future in mechanical engineering. The rest of his life would be spent playing referee in a kingdom full of chaotic goblins who never thought about girls—especially fairy girls—at all.

Luckily, Bellamy was busy juggling work, preparations for the masquerade, and studying for midterms. He'd barely seen her outside class. And with Hubble's theatre troupe constantly in rehearsals for the variety show they were putting on at the festival, Tinker didn't have any excuse to visit The Hallowed Bean.

He and Bellamy exchanged pleasantries in Physics every day, like they always did, but there were no more secret looks passed between them. Bellamy smiled at him, but Bellamy always smiled at him.

Are you okay? she'd written to him in her notebook.

Not really, he'd responded.

I'm here if you want to talk. I'm always here.

He *did* want to talk to Bellamy, but he wasn't sure where to start. Nor was he sure how to get two words out before having a complete emotional breakdown.

I'm always here.

Yes, he desperately wanted to talk to Bellamy, but it never seemed to be the right time. So it never happened, out loud or on paper. The only things written in their note-books from then on were classwork and test prep. There would be no more secret messages. No more sunshine. No more…

Tinker put a hand over his heart. He missed Bellamy already and he wasn't even gone yet.

He stayed in the shower a while longer, as if the hot water might burn away his longing for the fairy he could never have. But the water ran cold with the ache still present, so he gave up. He stepped out of the shower, dried his hair as best he could, wrapped a towel around his waist, and stepped back into the room he shared with Hubble.

He was not surprised to find Sam and Natalie there as well, chatting with Hubble around the coffee table.

"Hey, guys," Tinker said. "What's up?"

The trio looked up at him.

Natalie whistled. "Take my boots and call me Brittany."

"That's it." Hubble jumped up from the floor and crossed the room to where the Mantle of Mischief had been tossed on the dresser. "I'm checking this thing for radioactive spiders."

Sam leaned back against the sofa and tilted his head at Tinker. "So the goblin thing's only temporary? How's that work, exactly? I apparently know zero about your culture."

Tinker was confused. "I wasn't born a goblin, if that's what you mean. None of the Lost Boys are. But we all become goblins once we are welcomed into the horde."

"All except the Goblin King, am I right?" asked Hubble. "I mean, I've never met the guy, but I'm guessing he's easier on the eyes than the rest of you sad sacks."

Tinker had never really thought about it before. Of all the goblins, the king *did* look the most human. Since he was the one in charge of dealing with anyone who managed to infil-trate Goblin City from the outside world, it made sense for him to appear less threatening. That way, it was easier for him to convince people to leave...or stay, whatever the case may be. "Yeah, I guess. How did you—?"

Hubble shut the bathroom door and pulled Tinker in front of the full length mirror that hung on the back of it. For a moment, Tinker didn't recognize himself. He seemed tan from being outside so much—he didn't even know goblin skin could do that. Instead of sallow and yellow his skin was a rich olive brown, slightly darker in the places where bruises had left their marks. His hair was a much deeper shade of emerald, almost black. Except for his eyes, there was barely a hint of green about his person, and not a wart or a bump to be found. Anywhere. *Anywhere*. He looked. Twice.

Behind him in the mirror, Natalie fanned herself with a festival flyer. "I just can't even."

"Seriously, Natalie?" Sam groaned.

Hubble threw a handful of clothes at Tinker and pushed him back into the bathroom. "Dress yourself before you give Natalie the vapors."

"How long has this been going on?" Tinker called to Hubble through the door.

"Since your Lost Boys put that stupid tin hat on you," Hubble called back. "But the changes have been more... dramatic recently. You hadn't noticed?"

Tinker hadn't even thought about it. It wasn't like he ever spent a lot of time looking in the mirror. "No."

"Your shirts haven't felt smaller?"

"I guess not," said Tinker.

"And you haven't worn your glasses for two days. Didn't notice that either?"

Tinker's hands flew to his face. He *wasn't* wearing his glasses. But there was nothing wrong with his eyesight. He could see fine. He had half a mind to check the Mantle for radioactive spiders himself. He slid into his jeans—which had been much baggier before—and pulled on his NASA shirt. Hubble was right. It did feel snug.

"Just like Peter Parker," said Tinker.

"Or the Green Goblin," Hubble's voice answered. "A more appropriate analogy."

Fully dressed this time, Tinker opened the bathroom door once more. "Is this shirt okay?"

"Yes," Natalie said lustily.

"No," Sam and Hubble said in unison.

This time it was Sam who jumped up from the floor. "I'll

go see if one of the guys has something you can borrow."

"Try Finn first!" Tinker called after him, and then shrugged at the withering look Hubble gave him. "What? Finn at least has decent taste in concert tees." The shrug split the seam in his left sleeve.

Hubble sighed and rolled his eyes. Natalie cracked up.

Tinker tried to change the subject. "So what were you rocket scientists discussing before I rudely interrupted with my new and improved self?"

"One of the skits the drama club is doing for the festival is a comedic abridgment of *Romeo and Juliet*. I'm playing Juliet," Natalie said proudly.

"And Kwasi is Romeo," said Hubble. "I hate that guy."

"Be nice," said Natalie. "He's my date to the masquerade."

"He has to be," Hubble said. "He's Romeo to your Juliet. Just do us all a favor and don't end up dead by the end of the dance. I need you both in fighting form for the festival."

Tinker shook his head at both of them. "Who are you playing?" he asked Hubble.

"Mercutio, of course," Hubble said with a bow.

"You should see our costumes," said Natalie. "Ausrinne made them. She is a sewing *goddess*. We're going to look so fancy."

"And deadly," said Hubble.

"We're all wearing them tonight at the masquerade, to advertise for the festival," said Natalie. "What are you going to wear, Tinker?"

Tinker wanted to think about the dance he'd promised Bellamy about as much as he wanted to think about what happened when it was over. Both hurt too much. He started to shrug again, and then remembered the precarious state of his shirt. "I could always go as Spiderman. Just to be ironic."

"What? No," said Hubble. "It's a masquerade ball, bro. Not a Halloween party."

"There's a difference? I've never been to any parties at this school." Nor had Tinker ever wanted to attend such gatherings.

"One wears a costume at a Halloween party," said Natalie. "At a masquerade, people wear ballgowns and elaborate masks. It's a lot more formal."

"Like Zombie Prom?" Tinker asked.

"You guys have a Zombie Prom?" Natalie asked excitedly.

Hubble pinched an imaginary beard and scanned Tinker from head to toe. "You know, the theatre department might have just the thing for you. I'll get Ausrinne to tailor it."

"Now?" asked Natalie. "But the ball's *tonight*."

"Shouldn't be a problem."

"But you already owe her for…"

Hubble waved away Natalie's comment. "Yes, yes, I'm aware. Don't worry about it. Ausrinne knows I'll go to my grave owing her my soul. But we'll need to find him a mask."

"I'll take care of that," said Natalie. Tinker wondered if he should be worried about her enthusiasm, or the Hubble-like twinkle in her eye.

"We should go down right away so Ausrinne can take your measurements," said Hubble.

"Maybe she can fix my shirt," Tinker said offhandedly.

"Got one!" Sam yelled, brandishing a new shirt over his head. By the sheer volume of the thing, it appeared to belong to one of the gargoyles.

"No risk of that being too small," said Tinker.

Natalie turned around and faced the wall. "Quick, get changed so you can go see Ausrinne."

"You don't have to…" Tinker started.

"I've been ogled by enough guys," said Natalie. "Trust me. I know how uncomfortable it feels. But I'm not going to apologize for appreciating the sight of you earlier. Deal?"

Tinker laughed as he quickly changed into the massive

shirt. Having something that hung on his frame again felt strangely comforting. "Deal."

"All right, lover boy," Hubble said as he dragged Tinker out into the hall. "Let's get you to the costume department."

"We'll get started on the mask!" Natalie called after them.

"Can I take a nap first?" Tinker heard Sam ask his sister.

"Quick now." Hubble turned back briefly to glance at Tinker. "I wonder if we have time to get your hair trimmed, too. And what do your fingernails look like? Wait…don't show me. I can imagine."

Tinker self-consciously balled his hands into fists as he jogged after his best friend. "It sounds like you're giving me a makeover."

"I'm getting you ready for the performance of a lifetime," Hubble said as he turned the next corner. "The best LARP ever."

The last time Hubble had roped him into Live-Action Role Playing, Tinker had been forced to play the troll. "I don't know, Hubble…what if—*oof!*"

Tinker had run to catch up with Hubble, only to smack headlong into the guy running the opposite way around the same corner. Tinker saw only a flash of bright orange before falling straight onto his backside.

"Sorry, sorry," said the guy. "Totally my fault. Here, let me help you up."

Tinker clasped the proffered arm and stood back up, wobbling a bit before he found his balance. When he did, he found himself staring straight into Bellamy's eyes. But not Bellamy. Her brother. Asher.

As soon as Asher realized who he'd just helped to his feet, he dropped Tinker's arm like a hot potato. "Oh wow, Tinker! Dude, I'm so sorry. Are you okay?"

Tinker shook his head a bit to clear the cobwebs. He'd been surprised…thrown for a loop…but otherwise…

Suddenly, Hubble was back at his side. "It's fine, Asher. Go on. I'll make sure he gets to the nurse."

"Seriously. I am so, so sorry. I didn't realize... I mean, if anything happens to you, my sister will kill me."

"It's okay," Tinker said, still dazed. "I'll be good. I promise."

Asher's brow furrowed over those brilliant blue eyes, but he seemed reassured. He patted Hubble on the back and sped off.

"As fast as that guy goes, he should have been the one to get the wings in the family," Hubble said after Asher's retreating form. "Come on. Pit stop at the nurse. You know the drill."

"Wait," said Tinker.

"Sure. Sorry. Did the Flash knock you senseless? I should have given that fae fool a piece of my mind."

"Hubble, I feel fine."

"I'll give you a minute, but I don't want to wait too long before getting you to the nurse..."

"Hubble!" Tinker grabbed his friend's arms. "Look at me! I'm *fine*."

Hubble examined the forearm that Asher had touched. He squinted at Tinker's face, looked closely in one eye, and then the other. "I don't see a rash. There's no itching?"

"Nope."

Hubble still wasn't convinced. "No scratchy throat? No blurred vision?"

"Nothing."

"Maybe we should go to the nurse anyway, just to be sure..."

"Hubble, nothing is wrong with me. *Nothing*. I feel great. I feel..." The gravity of the situation finally began to sink in. If his goblinness *was* fading, it appeared that his fairy allergy was fading right along with it. "I feel...human."

His whole body filled with such pure happiness that it overwhelmed him. He lifted his head to the elaborately-painted ceiling and whooped from the joy of it all.

"Where do you think Bellamy is right now? The gym? The Bean?"

"Tinker, hold on a second."

"It doesn't matter. I'll check the gym first. I'll find her. And when I do…"

"Hey, mad man, are you listening to me?"

"…I'm going to lift her up in my arms…"

"Yeah, you're totally not hearing anything right now."

"…and give her the biggest hug that anybody ever gave anyone. And then…"

And then Hubble slapped him. Tinker shook his head again. "What the hell, Hubble?"

Hubble crooked his finger at Tinker. Tinker stooped until he was eye to eye with his so-called best friend. Then Hubble held up that same finger. Softly and evenly he said, "Parting is such sweet sorrow."

Tinker's nostrils flared in anger. "The Bard was full of crap," he said. "Parting isn't sweet. Parting sucks. And the Lost Boys are going to come and take me away any minute now. I can't guarantee that they'll wait until the masquerade."

"What?" said Hubble.

"Yeah." Tinker shrugged, and the gargoyle-sized shirt fell off one shoulder. "Fork and Willie have already come with a note from the Goblin King. I sent them away. Twice."

This time, it was Hubble who shook his head. "I wish you'd told me."

"Sorry."

"Apology accepted," said Hubble. "But it makes what I'm about to tell you all the more important. Are you listening to me?"

"Yes," Tinker said resignedly.

"Okay. So I may not have a lot of first-hand experience with love, but I have watched this storyline play out in performance after performance."

Tinker raised an eyebrow.

"Bellamy is a romantic," said Hubble. "And so are you, though you'd never admit it. You have to do the grand gesture. The most beautiful of all tragic endings. Wait until tonight…"

"Are you crazy? I don't want to wait another second."

"Think about it. She's bound to be wrapped up in last-minute setup for the ball, or she's already back at her room getting ready. Either way, you can't blow it all now and derail her. This is a very important night for her. And you."

"But what about the Lost Boys?"

"Don't worry about them. Sam and Natalie and I, your plucky band of misfits, will thwart the goblin horde. All you need to worry about is showing up at the ball, looking amazing—"

"I knew you just wanted to give me a makeover."

Hubble ignored him. "—and *then* you sweep that fairy off her feet. Give her the most romantic night of her life. One last, magical moment for you both to remember. Afterward, we'll let the goblins cart you away to the glorious stinking land of No Women Ever Again. What do you say?" Hubble held out his hand.

"Fine. I'll do it your way." Tinker shook his friend's hand and hoped the next few hours wouldn't be the death of him.

Giddy with power, Hubble practically skipped the rest of the way to the costume department, singing under his breath. As Tinker followed, he considered the one thing he hadn't told his roommate.

He was going to miss Hubble just as much as he was going to miss Bellamy.

5

Bellamy took a deep breath of the cool, crisp air and surveyed her handiwork. She had truly outdone herself this year. All the time and effort she had put in—so much more than previous masquerades—had certainly paid off.

It might have felt like a wet blanket outside, but in here the season had definitely changed. With the help of Kai and their tireless crew (and a generous splash of teacher-approved magic), the Harmswood gymnasium had been transformed into a winter wonderland. The edges of the room were now a dense wood of icy crystal trees with many winding, lantern-lit paths. The ceiling was a night sky dotted with twinkling stars and splashed with the Northern Lights. The dance floor was a large clearing of silvery white, circled by drifts of magically-induced snow. The scent of hot cider, roasted nuts, and spiced cakes drifted through the air from various old-fashioned wheeled "vendor carts" around the room.

But Bellamy's favorite part—the pièce de résistance—was a giant ice-pillar in the middle of the dance floor, on top of which sat an equally enormous snow globe. The scene inside the globe mirrored the shimmering majesty of the gym. In the center, two shadowy figures danced the night away amidst a flurry of glittery snow.

Encased in that crystal ball was the perfect night Bellamy would have wished for herself, had she been allowed such a wish.

"Bellamy!" Kai's voice pulled Bellamy out of her blissful, midwinter daydream. "Are you still here? The masquerade is supposed to start in an hour. It can't begin without you, and you're not even dressed!"

Bellamy turned to her friend. Kai was wearing a lovely blue and white gown. Her great golden headpiece was reminiscent of the Greek warrior goddess Athena. She was flanked by Finn, with his matching Apollo mask, and Owen, who wore a tux and a pair of fuzzy cat ears.

Kai wouldn't have to worry about having a partner with whom she could dance tonight away. If she got tired of one adoring young man, she could just switch to the other. Bellamy had...this gorgeous room, which she was about to share with the rest of Harmswood.

"My goodness, don't y'all look wonderful?" Bellamy's exhausted smile didn't quite reach her eyes.

As best friends tend to do, Kai heard what Bellamy wasn't saying. She dropped Finn's hand. "Guys, can you give us a minute? Go check on the drinks table or something."

"Will do," said Finn.

"I'll make sure there's ice," said Owen. "There's never enough ice at these sorts of things."

Kai raised her eyebrows dramatically as her dates walked away. "Owen's been stuck in the form of a stray cat for a hundred years. You gotta wonder how many of 'these sorts of things' he's really attended, bless his pompous heart."

Despite herself, Bellamy gave a half-laugh. Kai always could make her laugh.

"What's up with the sadness?" Kai asked bluntly. "It clashes with your...you know...everything."

Bellamy glanced at the clock. There wasn't enough time to pour her heart out again. Even if there had been, Kai had already heard it a hundred times. Since the moment she'd realized she was in love with Tinker, Bellamy had begun to see him differently. He looked taller—if that were possible—and handsomer, broader of chest and fuller of heart. Her heart. Her longing for him had grown so much that she was fit to burst, but there was nothing she could do about it, and Tinker seemed determined to keep her at arm's length.

"You'll tell me I'm bein' silly."

"Between Finn and Owen, I could start a business in silly. Hit me."

As usual, Bellamy could hide nothing from her best friend. "I'm...scared."

"About Tinker," Kai surmised. "About the dance he promised you."

Bellamy nodded. "It's just...I keep tellin' myself that if the ball never starts, then it never has to end." And then Tinker would never have to leave.

"The clock never stops ticking, Bell. This ball is going to happen whether you want it to or not."

The masquerade was going to happen. Bellamy and Tinker would have their dance. And then, someday very soon, the goblins would come for Tinker and Bellamy's already fragile heart would break into a million pieces.

Life would happen, and no wish or spell or bleeding heart could stop it.

"You've been avoiding him," Kai pointed out. "That's not going to make his leaving any easier."

"I know," said Bellamy.

"I've been trying to imagine that he's just going away for winter break. And that he won a scholarship to a really exclusive college or something."

"But he didn't," said Bellamy. "Tinker's not goin' off to chase his dreams. He's leavin' Harmswood and never comin' back." She shook her head. "Sorry, I don't know what's wrong with me. It's stupid. It's not like we could have had a future anyway. Besides…he's gonna be a king! I should be happy for him, just like everyone else. This should be a happy time for all of us. I have no business ruinin' that."

Kai held out her hand and Bellamy took it. "Can I tell you something? As your best friend?"

Bellamy couldn't imagine ever being upset at Kai, for anything. "Of course."

"You are allowed to feel however you want to feel, nonsense or not. You are allowed to be sad, mad, scared, and anything else that comes along. You are allowed to grieve. Someone you love is going away, and that's just going to be terrible."

"But I don't want to grieve yet," said Bellamy. "I want tonight to be wonderful. For you and me, for Tinker, for everyone."

"If anyone could make that happen, it's you," said Kai. "Just look around this place! You have done some amazing work here. The entire school is going to be in awe, and they're going to have the time of their lives. It will be a night we all remember."

Bellamy clasped her hands together. Kai always knew the right thing to say to her. "Really?"

"Really. But you've worked so hard these past few weeks to hide the pain of losing Tinker…heck, you've worked your whole life to hide the pain of being different."

Bellamy smirked. "I forget how well you know me."

"So…how about you let yourself off the hook?"

"What do you mean?"

Kai put her hands on her hips. "What I mean, Bellamy Larousse, chair of the Midwinter Masquerade decorating committee, is that you are fired."

Bellamy couldn't believe her ears. "*What?*"

Kai the Goddess waved her finger in the air. "I hereby officially decree that you are no longer in charge of insuring everyone else's happiness. It is not your job, do you hear me? As of right now, you are allowed—no, *ordered*—to be selfish. It's about time you let your friends lift *you* up for a change."

Bellamy felt tears well up behind her eyes, but she refused to shed them.

"And I want you to do me a favor tonight," said Kai. "As your best and truest friend."

"Anythin'," she managed to say without weeping.

"Stay. No matter how lonely or sad or frightened you get, stay at the masquerade. Stay on the dance floor with us. If there's an emergency that needs to be addressed, let me deal with it. Allow yourself to be admired. Play hostess only until some boy asks you to dance…because he will. And if no one comes to dance with you soon enough, I'll be your partner. Or I'll send Finn."

"I don't need a pity dance."

"You'll be the one pitying Finn, once he's stepped on your toes a few times."

Bellamy could not avoid the name that hung heavy on her heart. "And…Tinker?"

"Oh, Bell, Tinker loves you so much. *Let him.* Whether he can touch you or not. Love him back. Enjoy being together. It's all right."

Bellamy looked to the glowing, star-filled ceiling, willing

gravity to pull the threatening tears back down inside her. "Saying goodbye is gonna hurt so much."

"If I could spare you the pain of it, I would."

"He promised me one dance." Bellamy took a shuddering breath. "But what if it's only one?"

"Then make it a good one. But maybe try not to put him in the hospital."

"Upon my honor, I swear to do my very best. *Not to*," Bellamy added quickly. "You know what I mean."

"I do." Kai chuckled and kissed Bellamy's cheek. "Now, off with you! We have a masquerade to begin!"

With the spring back in her step, Bellamy raced up the stairs to her room in the girls' wing. Lian was already there, dressed in a floor-length, violet silk wrap dress with bright pink flowers along the seams. A delicate strand of ivy and varying colors of glitter made up an organic half-mask that enhanced Lian's dark eyes. She looked to be putting some finishing touches on her face with a brush that she dropped the moment Bellamy walked in.

"Fairy girl, where have you been?"

"I know, I'm sorry. I got caught up in…well, it doesn't matter. It's late and I don't have much time. Will you help me?"

"Of course! But first you have to open the giant box your mom sent. I'm sure it's your dress…I can't wait to see it!"

Bellamy smiled, though she was a little confused. She knew how much Lian loved surprises, and Mrs. Larousse often sent tailored clothes for Bellamy to add to her closet, making her meager wardrobe all the more special. But her mother usually sent a message beforehand so that Bellamy knew to expect a package. In fact, she'd just had a call from home yesterday, and Mom hadn't dropped so much as a hint about this. Had she known how important this masquerade was for Bellamy? Had Merri said something? Or Asher?

The giant white box was wrapped with a sky blue silk ribbon. A slip of paper under the bow read: *For Bellamy. Love, Mom.*

Bellamy furrowed her brow. "That's not my mother's handwritin'."

"Well, it's got your name on it, and you're the only 'Bellamy' at Harmswood," Lian said impatiently. "She probably bought it for you online and the delivery person wrote the card for her. Like when you send flowers."

"Maybe," said Bellamy, though she hoped that wasn't the case. Her parents couldn't afford such extravagance. But she pulled at the silk ribbon anyway and opened the box, before Lian did it for her.

Both the girls drew in their breath at once.

Bellamy picked up the iridescent white chiffon by the sleeves and gently lifted it out of the box. The dress just kept going and going…like something out of a movie.

"Put it on!" Lian said excitedly. "We'll examine it properly once it's on you. There's no time to waste."

Bellamy glanced at the clock—she had little more than half an hour to spare. "Let me rinse off." She pulled a few fresh underthings from a drawer and vanished into the bathroom. "I'll be right out."

Bellamy pinned up her hair and washed her face quickly. Then she set herself to the most important task: removing all the fairy dust on her wings that she could reach. If there had been sufficient time to dry she would have completely immersed herself in the shower, but she couldn't show up at the ball in a fairy tale gown with disastrously limp wings.

Within minutes, it looked as if a rainbow had exploded in the bathroom. There was enough loose fairy dust on the floor to make an elephant fly.

"Bellamy, aren't you done yet?"

"Almost there." Satisfied, Bellamy rinsed her skin off once

more with the last clean towel. She wanted to be as harmless to Tinker as humanly—fairy-ly—possible. She slid on her underthings and emerged so that Lian could help her put on the dress. "I have a pair of fancy gloves I wore to the Spring Social, don't let me forget them."

"I won't," Lian said as she pushed the box aside and let the dress spill out.

The back looked like it was cut daringly low, but once Bellamy pulled it on and Lian fastened her in, she realized that the drop perfectly accommodated her wings. The sleeves were full at the top and then tight at the elbow, tapering to a point down the backs of her hands. The snug waistline accentuated the fullness of the skirt, which fell to the floor in glittering silver and white waves that covered her toes.

Lian stepped back and sighed. "It's magical. Simply magical."

And it was. Bellamy had thought the same thing about the masquerade decorations, similarly wintry silver and white. The pureness of the cloth highlighted the iridescence in her now almost colorless wings. Somehow, her mother had chosen the perfect costume for her to lead tonight's festivities.

"I have some white sandals—they're a little old, but they'll match well enough," said Bellamy.

"I'll fetch them," said Lian.

Bellamy moved to the mirror. "And now I'm wishin' Kai and I hadn't streaked my hair with all those colors this summer." She loved her rainbow hair more than anything, but against the beautiful dress, the fading tresses looked a bit haggard.

"Let me worry about your hair." Sandals in hand, Lian examined the flowerpots on the windowsill. "Just give me a second."

Bellamy scanned the top of her dresser. The ballgown had a sweetheart neckline made for a necklace, but every piece of jewelry Bellamy owned would have paled in contrast to this dress. Except… Bellamy snatched up the blue silk ribbon from the dress box and threaded it through the hole of the heart-shaped piece of tin that had dropped from Tinker's Mantle of Majesty. Tinker himself had called it cheap, and maybe it looked a little silly as a necklace, but Bellamy didn't mind. Maybe by wearing it, Tinker would realize just how much she cared about him.

On the off chance he didn't know already.

She tied the long ribbon around her neck and neatly snipped off the ends, then sat down before the mirror. Lian appeared behind her with a handful of wildflowers.

Bellamy gaped. "Snowdrops? Do you want to get suspended?" Among the flower fairy community, it was frowned upon to bloom wildflowers out of season.

Lian scoffed. "If anyone gives us a hard time about the galanthus—which they won't—I'll blame our bathroom full of fairy dust."

"Sorry about that," said Bellamy. "I promise I'll clean up when we get back."

"You don't have to be sorry about anything," said Lian. "This is a big night! Now hold still while I fix your hair."

Bellamy closed her eyes as Lian brushed her hair and then threaded her fingers through it, twisting and pinning. The effect was incredibly soothing. Bellamy took a deep breath and forced herself to relax. She remembered Kai's words: *Be selfish. Let your friends lift you up for a change.*

"There," Lian said all too quickly. "Finished."

Bellamy opened her eyes. Her hair had been expertly twisted at the temples and secured with butterfly clips and snowdrops. Here and there, her rainbow streaks added a subtle flash of color. A few loose tendrils of honey gold curled down her back. The style was elegant in its simplicity.

"Lian, you are a genius!"

Her roommate chuckled. "You forget that I have almost as many sisters as you do. I've had lots of practice! Now, let's make you a mask. How daring do you feel?"

Bellamy answered honestly. "In this dress? With this hair? I feel like I could conquer the world."

Lian's grin was wicked this time. "Excellent. Tilt your head back and close your eyes again while I fetch your pillow."

Bellamy did as instructed. "Because you're gonna smother me with it?"

Lian giggled from across the room. "Hush!"

Bellamy heard Lian unzip the pillow—she forced herself to banish the silly image of being tarred and feathered. She felt Lian draw a line above her brows with something cool, before pressing her fingertips along its length.

"Hold still while that dries," said Lian. "I'm going to glitter you up a bit."

"Good." Glitter always boosted Bellamy's spirits.

Lian gently applied Bellamy's makeup along her eyelids and up to her temples. She felt a dab of something on the apples of her cheeks, and a sprinkle of something over her skin in general. Lian pressed the line above her eyebrows with her fingers again, blowing on it for good measure.

"Perfect timing," said Lian. "I'm going to let you do your own lipstick. We only have about five minutes to fly back downstairs, so don't dawdle."

Bellamy opened her eyes and gasped. The line Lian had drawn had been some sort of glue, into which she had pressed some downy feathers from her pillow and a few rhinestone crystals. The result was a very natural-looking tiara. Coupled with the rest of her silver and white glitter makeup, it made a gorgeous mask. "You really are an artist," she breathed.

"Yeah, well, don't tell my parents. They want me to be a doctor." She pointed at the clock. "Now we only have four minutes. Lip gloss and let's go!"

Bellamy quickly applied a shimmer to her lips and sped after Lian. Together, they raced down the halls and jumped down the stairs. Bellamy felt the wind in her face and smiled into it. She was Cinderella running to the ball, instead of away from it.

They slipped through the door of the gym just as the band began playing the school song. Every major event started with the Harmswood anthem. Bellamy and Lian joyfully lifted their voices along with the rest of the assembly.

Sun and sand and sea and sky
Though Harmswood years go flying by
Rock and fire, wind and rain
This bond will bring us home again

Bellamy scanned the crowd. She caught Kai's eye—her best friend gave her a thumbs up. She spotted her sister Merri, too. Merri also seemed to be looking for someone… someone that Bellamy noticed first. Half-hidden in the trees was Polaris Brighton, Merri's matchmaking partner-in-crime and lifelong crush.

Good, thought Bellamy. *If Bright is here, Merri will be on her best behavior.*

There seemed to be no sign of Tinker, but with so many students wearing masks, it was hard to tell. She thought about all the things she had promised Kai and tried not to be disappointed.

For one, for all
The brave and true

Our Harmswood family
Through and through!

The end of the school song was met with applause, and then cheers as a well-timed spell rained bubbles from the sky. Bellamy's heart soared. The Midwinter Masquerade had begun!

6

Tinker fidgeted as he waited for Hubble to arrive with his suit for the masquerade. He glanced from the window to the clock and back again…they were already late. Tinker flipped the latch and slid the window open, wincing as the thick outdoor heat assaulted his face and took his breath away. From the opposite end of campus, he could just make out a low chorus of voices singing the Harmswood alma mater.

He might not have been a regular attendee at school functions—a fact he'd give anything right now to go back and change—but he knew they always started this way. The voices raised in song were like a spell lifted into the night. He actually liked the lyrics, filled with their well-meaning camaraderie, even if they were a total lie. Sure, most of Harmswood loved him now that he was heir to a throne they knew nothing about, but Tinker knew who his loyal companions were. He could count them on one hand.

"For one for all, the brave and true," Tinker whispered along in the oppressive heat. He'd never been much of a singer.

"Are you nuts? It's a sauna out there! Close the window!"

It never got this hot in Goblin City. Tinker wasn't sure if that made him happy or sad. Either way, he obeyed Hubble and twisted the latch shut again. "Where have you been?"

The answer was obvious: not only had Hubble fetched Tinker's costume, but he'd also completed his own wardrobe change. Hubble was now bedecked in black from head to toe: shoes, slacks, button-down shirt and bolero tie. He wore a flat-top hat with a wide brim, a long cape that swirled around his knees, and a wickedly-pointed, bone-white plague doctor mask.

"Wow! What are you supposed to be?"

"I am the Black Death."

Tinker couldn't see Hubble's face, but he could easily imagine the pompous smirk beneath the mask.

"Romeo and Juliet is all about death," Hubble added.

"Which I see you've decided to take literally."

Hubble removed the mask for ease of speaking. "It's about staying true to the art. Especially when it comes to Shakespeare."

Tinker held up a hand. Hubble could go on for hours about Shakespeare, and Tinker was ready to jump out of his skin with anticipation. "They've already sung the song. We need to hurry!"

The kobold's shrug frustrated Tinker even more. "We're supposed to be late. That's the only way to make a grand entrance."

Tinker grit his teeth and forced a smile. It was true; Hubble certainly knew a thing or two about grand entrances.

"Don't give me any grief." His roommate gave a pompous smirk. "I just scared the mess out of your little goblin brother in this getup."

Tinker's whole body went tense. "Which brother?"

"The one you call Snot," Hubble said as he unzipped the garment bag. "He was carrying another note from the Goblin King about how you needed to 'come at once or else,' blah blah blah. I told him I had unfinished business with you. And I might have been a little intimidating."

Poor Snot. After seeing Hubble in that get-up, the kid would probably have nightmares for weeks. Tinker vowed to make it up to him later. "Thank you."

"Hey, I told you I would deal with anyone who came to fetch you, and I will. You will get through this night, or my name isn't Hubble G. Hobson."

Tinker smiled to himself. He knew better than to ask what the G stood for. Definitely something he would miss teasing Hubble about for the rest of his days. And then Tinker caught a glimpse of what had been hidden inside the garment bag.

"Are those ruffles? No. N-O. So much no. *All* the no. Ruffles were not in the deal."

"I said you were going to have to trust me. So trust me."

Tinker began to rethink the whole "missing Hubble" thing. "Dude, I'd follow you over the Falls, but I am not wearing a costume from…what…*The Phantom of the Opera?*"

Hubble rolled those extremely-blue eyes of his. "Get out of your own brain and think like a romantic, my friend. Women have loved every guy that has ever worn this suit."

"It's a school dance, Hubble. Not one of your precious plays."

"This is a *masquerade*." Hubble raised a finger. "And all the world's a stage. Now go put this on and yell at me afterward, willya? Sam and Natalie will be here any minute. And we're late, remember?"

Tinker knew that if he didn't do this one thing for Hubble, as ridiculous as it was, he'd never forgive himself.

Plus, even if there was time, there wasn't anything in his wardrobe even close to decent enough to wear instead.

He put on the pressed black trousers and buttoned up the shirt that belonged on a historical romance cover. Hubble helped him as he slid the jacket on over it—there were even ruffles on the shirt's *sleeves*. And the jacket had *tails*. To be fair, it all did fit like a glove. That Ausrinne had some serious talent.

Tinker felt his body threaten to sweat beneath the layers. "I sure hope it's cold in the gym, because it's certainly not in these clothes."

"Beauty is pain," Hubble said as Tinker buttoned up the jacket. Hubble stood back to look over his work, then hopped up on the closest bed and tousled Tinker's hair. "There. Perfect."

"You're kidding."

Just then, Natalie and Sam burst through the door. "You guys! Wait until you see..." Natalie stopped dead in her tracks. "Whoa. Move over, Tom Hiddleston."

Natalie had on a crimson sheath dress, the sleeves of which made her seem as though she'd been dipped in blood. Her headdress was a skull face, crowned by a towering mass of red feather quills.

Tinker smiled. Maybe the ruffles weren't so terrible after all. "You don't look half bad yourself."

Natalie pointed to herself, and then Hubble. "Get it? Red Death and Black Death. Kwasi's going to be Osiris. Egyptian God of the Dead."

"Fitting," said Tinker.

"If Kwasi expects us to address him as 'your highness,' he is sadly mistaken," Hubble said curtly.

"I'll cut him up into pieces so small that he'll have to find an Isis to put him back together again," said Natalie.

Tinker shook his head. "I am really going to miss you guys."

"Don't talk about leaving," said Sam. His simple black mask was topped with a floppy pirate hat. "I'm not ready to deal with it yet."

"We at least have to leave this room," Tinker said impatiently.

"Here." Sam handed Tinker a mask as they finally walked out the door. It was a work of art: a theatrical rendition of a menacing goblin's face, complete with dark green skin and horns that gleamed gold in the right light. There were even a few warts on its nose.

"Wow, that's…intense," said Tinker.

"It's brilliant!" cried Hubble.

"You don't think it will scare Bellamy away, do you?"

"Brother, if you haven't scared Bellamy off after all these years, she's not going anywhere," said Hubble.

Kwasi was waiting for them by the gymnasium doors. He wore a sleeveless kaftan that showed off the gold bands around his wrists and muscular upper arms. Above his eyes, his mask became a tall Egyptian crown, complete with ostrich feathers. "About time, Juliet," he said in that deep voice of his.

"Shut up, Romeo." Natalie placed her hand inside Kwasi's elbow. "I was totally worth waiting for."

"Is the coast clear?" asked Hubble.

Sam peeked through the door. "Looks good to me," he said.

Tinker adjusted the goblin mask over his face. "I don't think I can breathe."

"Yes you can." Hubble winked at him before pulling down his own mask. "Now let's rock this thing."

Sam took one side of the doors; Tinker took the other. At

Sam's nod, they pulled them both open. Hubble strode in, with Natalie and Kwasi a few paces behind. Tinker immediately began scanning the ornate room full of students.

Hubble threw his arms up in the air. Two small balls flew from the sleeves of his black cloak, exploding with a quick bang—a trick Tinker had rigged for Hubble years ago, still dramatic as ever. A shower of rainbow bubbles floated down to the snow and popped around Hubble's feet, making it look as if he'd just slaughtered a unicorn.

"HEAR YE, HEAR YE!" Hubble's words rang out clearly and articulately from behind his mask. Clever kobold had more than one spell handy tonight. The DJ brought the music to a screeching halt. "Two households, both alike in dignity"—Hubble motioned to Natalie and Kwasi in turn —"in fairest Harmswood, where we lay our scene. From ancient grudge break to new mutiny, where civil blood makes civil hands unclean... The Frozen Fest Players proudly present: *Romeo and Juliet!*"

Natalie and Kwasi bowed to the crowd. The music immediately started back up again—a waltz this time. Osiris and the Red Death lead the charge in perfectly executed choreography.

Tinker searched frantically for Bellamy. How could she be so hard to find? He normally had a sixth sense that alerted him to wherever she was in the room. But in the dim pseudo-starlight, with everyone's colorful outfits and faces obscured by masks, even Bellamy's distinctive fairy wings were hard to pinpoint.

Suddenly, a young woman in a periwinkle gown blocked his view. Her short, cornsilk hair made an angelic halo around her head. "Hey there, tall, green and handsome. May I have this dance?"

"I'm actually looking for—" Tinker started to say, but the woman wasn't taking no for an answer. She took up his left hand in her right glove and put his other hand at her waist. Then she waltzed him into the throng of dancers that circled around an oversized, snow globe-topped pillar of ice. Tinker tripped a couple of times before he figured out how to match her steps, but he caught on quickly enough. The woman smiled at his efforts. Her eyes twinkled behind her lavender mask. Her very familiar, kaleidoscope blue eyes.

"Are you related to Bellamy?" Tinker asked. The full goblin mask muffled his voice.

"A penny for the smart boy," she said. "I'm Merri. Bellamy's meddling older sister."

Tinker guessed that she wanted him to ask her about the meddling, but he was far more interested in her sister's current whereabouts. His heart leapt. "Have you seen Bellamy? I owe her a dance, and I—"

Merri took a few steps backward, expertly making it look like Tinker had been the one to spin her around. "She's over there, dancing with my old friend Brighton. Big, poofy, cake-topper gown. Can't miss her."

Once Tinker had Bellamy in his sights, he wondered how he'd missed her at all. Bedecked in silvery white with those diaphanous wings, she looked like a snow sprite. Or Glinda from *The Wizard of Oz*. Or a princess who'd just stepped right out of a fairy tale.

His princess.

Her beautiful hair had been pulled into some fancy updo. As she laughed at something her black-haired dance partner said, one of the white flowers slipped out and fluttered to the ground. He wanted nothing more in the world right now than to rescue that tiny bud and return it to his true love.

"If you'll excuse me," Tinker said, but Merri wouldn't let him pull away.

"Not so fast, hot stuff," she said. "All in good time. You and I need to have a little chat first."

Bellamy was *right there*, and Tinker was about ready to burn the gymnasium down if he didn't touch her soon. "About what?" he asked gruffly.

"Gee, I don't know." Merri narrowed her eyes at him. "Maybe let's start with my little sister, and your intentions."

Tinker sighed. "She is a dream I dare not dream." He wasn't sure why he suddenly sounded like Hubble after a day on the stage—maybe it was the mask, or the outfit—but the pretty words sounded like he felt, so he didn't mind too much.

"Why not?"

Tinker made a face at Merri, even though she couldn't see it. "I'm sure you already know the details of my situation. Even if goblins and fairies could be together"—no sense in ruining that surprise before he found out if his allergy to Bellamy had truly vanished once and for all—"I have to leave. Soon." *Forever*, he didn't say.

"But you love her," Merri said matter-of-factly.

Tinker didn't ask her how she knew, for it was true enough. "I would give up my kingdom for her," he said.

Merri cupped the goblin mask's cheek in her gloved hand as if it were Tinker's own face. "Poor dearest," she said wistfully. "I'm familiar with the heartache that comes from pining away for one person for a very long time."

"Got any advice?" Tinker asked.

"Treasure every moment you have together," said Merri. "No matter how bad or good or weird or magical. Those are the moments that help you survive all the other ones."

Tinker tried to ask Merri what she meant by "weird or magical," but she stepped backward again, lifting her arms and spinning them both around like a top. When Tinker stopped twirling and settled into dance position again, the person in his arms wasn't Merri anymore.

It was Bellamy.

His right hand touched the waist of her ball gown. Her right hand rested lightly in his.

They were holding hands.

And she wasn't wearing gloves. And he wasn't breaking out in hives.

His heart did jumping jacks.

Beside them, Merri and her old friend Brighton danced gaily off into the crowd as if nothing had happened.

Tinker forgot to breathe for so long that he tripped. But when he regained his balance, it was Bellamy who apologized.

"Sorry about my sister," she said. "She can be a bit of a…flibbertigibbet."

Tinker wasn't sure what to say. Did Bellamy not realize it was him? She couldn't have, or she wouldn't still be holding his hand. Even with the goblin mask, the costume Hubble had chosen for Tinker was just crazy enough to fool his oldest, dearest friend.

She was still holding his hand.

Tinker tried to remember to breathe, and not trip again. He was dancing with Bellamy. *Finally.* He wanted to freeze this moment in his memory, just like Merri had advised, so that he could relive it for the rest of his pathetic life. He concentrated on Bellamy's beautiful face so hard that the rest of the room blurred and faded away.

He really should say something. But what?

Bellamy's steps began to slow. "You don't have to dance with me if you don't want to."

Tinker almost burst out laughing, but he caught himself. He didn't want to offend her. He stepped backward and spun her around, the way Merri had just taught him. "I promised you a dance, so you're getting a dance."

Bellamy's brow furrowed at Tinker's muffled response. It

took her a few more heartbeats to examine his mask and realize what it was…and whose hand she held.

A few more precious heartbeats.

"Oh, god, *Tinker*?" Bellamy gasped. She tore her soft, warm hand out of his and Tinker winced behind the mask. "I had no idea! My gloves…where are my gloves?"

"Bellamy, wait."

The pitch of her voice got higher and higher. "I must have left them in the room! Lian and I were so excited about the dress that we forgot the gloves…oh, Tinker, I'm so sorry!"

"Bellamy, hold on—"

Bellamy turned to run from him, but there was nowhere to go. The rest of the gym *had* faded away. It seemed that they were now—somehow—trapped together inside the snow globe at the top of the ice pillar.

"No!" she cried. "This can't be happenin'. I'm gonna *kill* Merri and Bright." Bellamy pounded her fists on the frosted glass. "Help! We need the nurse immediately!" But neither the music nor sea of dancers below them stopped.

Tinker removed his goblin mask. "Bellamy."

"I don't think they can hear us." Bellamy slapped the glass again. "HELP!"

"BELLAMY, STOP!" Tinker wanted to grab her, but he didn't want to touch her again without asking, and he didn't want her to freak out even more. He tried to remain as calm as he could, even though his insides were electric. "Please. Just…*look*."

She turned back to him, her face a wreck of concern, and he fell in love with her all over again. He showed her his hand, the one she'd been holding. There were no welts, no bumps, no redness of any sort.

"Is it a spell?"

Tinker shook his head.

She reached out to touch his fingers with her own, stopping just short of actual contact. "You don't feel sick?"

Tinker resisted the urge to close the distance himself. "I don't think I've ever felt more perfect than I do right now."

Eyes wide, she slid her fingers slowly in between his until their palms touched. The movement was tender and gentle, unlike the storm raging beneath Tinker's skin. He wanted his body, his lips, to do what their hands were doing right now, but he restrained himself. Over the years, Tinker had watched too many people take advantage of Bellamy's personal space. He wasn't going to be another.

And then she launched herself at him.

Bellamy's arms circled his neck as she hugged him tightly. It surprised Tinker so much that he side-stepped, fumbling a bit, not quite knowing how to hug her back. He settled on placing one arm around her waist and letting the other stretch up between her wings. The skin of her back was so soft; the muscles beneath, incredibly defined. Tinker knew that Bellamy was strong—he'd watched her perform all those crazy gymnastic stunts for her cheer routines. He'd considered the biology of a fairy's wings, the physical power required to lift a body and fly, but he'd never imagined he'd feel it firsthand.

He never wanted it to end.

Her hair smelled of warmth and wildflowers. All around them, the globe's magical glitter snow continued its perpetual fall. Tinker could feel her laugher against his chest. At least, he hoped it was laughter. He didn't want to stop hugging her, but he had to know... "Bellamy? Are you laughing or crying?"

"Both." Her breath caressed the curve of his neck and Tinker's knees felt weak.

He chuckled a little. "I know how you feel."

She arched her back enough so that she could see his face,

but her arms never left his chest, and her feet still seemed to have no desire to touch the ground. This close, at this height, Tinker got a good look at her odd necklace.

"Is that... Bell, are you wearing a piece of the Goblin Mantle?"

Bellamy's hand flew to the heart-shaped bit of tin around her neck and she blushed. Tinker's suit suddenly felt unbearably warm. "I know you told me to throw them away, but I just couldn't. Kai had already fixed them, and...well...this one was my favorite." Her eyes twinkled. "One goblin's trash is another fairy's treasure."

He wished he'd had the means to give her something more appropriate to remember him by: diamonds or pearls or precious gems. But he could see how much it meant to her. Bellamy didn't care that it was a tiny scrap of metal. She cared that it was a part of him.

"On me, it was worthless," said Tinker. "On you, it is the most priceless treasure in the goblin kingdom." And it was. Because that was just the magic of Bellamy.

Tenderly, she touched his cheek. "I totally know how this happened," she said with complete sincerity.

"You mean my magical, hypo-allergenic upgrade to Tinker 2.0? Pretty sure it was the Mantle of Meshugenah. At least, that's my and Hubble's best guess."

A grin spread across Bellamy's face as she shook her head. Two more white flowers fell from her hair, but Tinker let them go. "It was the fairy dust."

"What?" He had no idea what she was talking about.

"In the Bean. Before your goblin brothers arrived. I accidentally dosed you with dust and you sneezed like crazy."

"I remember that part. But I don't remember..."

"You had just asked if I could turn you into a super-strong chick magnet." She smacked his shoulder playfully. "Looks like it worked."

Unable to contain his joy, Tinker spun them both around. Bellamy threw her arms in the air, spread her wings, and turned her face up to the magic snow. When she came back down to him, he could see tear streaks in the glitter on her face. He reluctantly moved one of his hands from around her so that he could wipe them away.

"Don't cry, fairy girl."

Bellamy closed her eyes and turned her sparkling cheek into his palm. Tinker felt ill. Not because he was a goblin touching a fairy, but because at some point he would have to stop touching Bellamy, and it was going to hurt more than he'd ever hurt before.

"No matter what happens," he said, "no matter where I go or how long I'm gone, always remember how much I love you."

She nodded, ever so slightly. "Remember that I love you too."

And then he kissed her, because he refused to waste one more minute of his life not kissing her. Her lips were soft beneath his...and then hungry. Her hands clutched at his arms and then slid up into his hair. He kissed her once, twice, three times...over and over again...making up for lost time. Bellamy did the same, meeting his fervor with equal enthusiasm. There, happily trapped in that perfect crystal ball, they lost themselves in each other.

And then the world exploded.

A bright light split the sky, blinding him. Bellamy's body was ripped from his—or he from hers. Tinker fell through a dark, freezing chasm of nothingness. He blinked several times, unable to tell if his eyes were open or closed. He screamed but no sound emerged.

When light finally began to return, Tinker found himself kneeling on a stone floor. His body shivered uncontrollably. His stomach revolted and he gagged with sickness, but nothing came out. He stared at that floor for a few deep breaths. He knew where he was. He knew what he would see when he finally looked up: Maker Deng, staring down at him from his great tin throne.

"I got tired of waiting," said the Goblin King. "Welcome back, brother."

7

One minute Bellamy was kissing Tinker, the boy she loved with all her heart, and who loved her right back. It was the best minute of her life.

In the next, she was falling through the air in an explosion of light and crystal. She managed to spread her dustless wings, barely catching herself before she faceplanted into the icy dance floor. Unearthly sirens sounded from every direction, howling through the gymnasium so loudly that even the ghost students covered their ears. Bellamy doubled over as the chaos whirled around her, spitting out mouthfuls of glitter and snow that had once fallen inside the globe.

"Everyone, please exit the gymnasium in an orderly fashion," she heard Professor Van Zant's voice call out above the din. "This is not a drill."

Bellamy wanted to search the rubble for Tinker, but she couldn't seem to get her legs to obey her. Nor could she stop trembling. They'd been together when the explosion happened, and Tinker didn't have wings. But she didn't see his injured body in the immediate vicinity, so he must have been well enough to walk away from the blast...

"Kwasi, if you please," she heard someone else say. Natalie?

Two dark arms ringed with gold bands lifted Bellamy off the floor and carried her out of the gym. She might have protested if she'd been able to find her voice. Where was Tinker? Where was Kai? Where was her sister? What had happened?

There must have been a glitchy spell in the snow globe. Or the pillar. Bellamy had been too distracted to triple check that all the spells and wards the teachers had woven into the decorations were safe and sound.

This is all my fault, she wanted to say, but couldn't.

Kwasi carried her all the way into the courtyard. Sirens echoed off every ancient stone facade. Snow was still falling all around her.

The heat wave had broken.

Try as she might, Bellamy couldn't find the will to be excited about the weather. This sky had no stars. This snow didn't have glitter in it. She was cold. So very, very cold. Her bare wings didn't help with their lack of insulation.

"You can put her there, thank you," said Natalie.

Bellamy was lowered to a low stone wall. "She's shaking like a leaf."

Natalie looked at Kwasi's sleeveless kaftan and wrinkled her nose. "Hubble!" she called out into the night.

Bellamy didn't want Hubble. She wanted Kai, if anyone. And Tinker. Above all, she wanted Tinker here beside her. He would put his arms around her, now that he could. He would hold her close and tell her that everything would be all right.

But it wasn't all right. Ear-shattering alarms didn't go off when everything was all right.

Bellamy wanted to ask where Tinker was, and if he was safe, but she knew.

She knew he was gone.

Bellamy lifted her hand to the heart-shaped piece of tin at her throat and clung to the cold metal, as if somehow it could tell her otherwise.

A short figure in black emerged from the shrubbery. "I'm here," Hubble's voice said from behind the sharply-pointed mask.

"Hubble, give me your cloak. She's in shock. Kwasi, see if you can find Kai. Or Bellamy's sister." Natalie paused. "Preferably Kai."

Only someone as strong-willed as Natalie could get a natural trickster like Kwasi to obey her command with no funny business. Paranormal or not, Natalie was a good person to have in a crisis. Bellamy felt the cloak settle over her shoulders, flattening her wings down her back. It did little to stave off the chill. She remembered Tinker's warm hands on her skin, pulling her to him. The pressure of his lips on hers...and then nothing but cold. She shuddered again.

Natalie crouched before Bellamy. "Tinker was with you in the snow globe, wasn't he?"

Bellamy was glad that Natalie had asked a question she could answer, and not something silly like, "Are you okay?" But before Bellamy could find her voice to reply, Hubble answered for her.

"Yes," Hubble said, with a mouth that was his own now, and not some ibis-beaked skull's. "They were up there together. But it wasn't supposed to end this way."

Bellamy studied Hubble's silver-skinned face, now ashen gray. The only reason he would have said such a thing was if he had orchestrated any—or all—of tonight's events. The drama club's entrance. Natalie and Kwasi leading a waltz. Merri and Brighton, matchmaking them right into that snow globe. That romantic Victorian costume Tinker never would have chosen on his own, the artistic goblin mask, and…

"The dress," Bellamy whispered through chattering teeth. "*You* sent the dress." That answered the question of the strange handwriting.

"You sent her a dress?" Natalie grabbed the shimmering white material of Bellamy's overskirt in both hands. "*This* was the thing you had Ausrinne toiling away on? I thought her plate was full because of our festival costumes. What are you, some kind of fairy godmother now?"

"I am a *director*," Hubble said with a flourish that would have been a great deal more dramatic if Natalie hadn't requisitioned his cape. Bellamy pulled the cloth tighter around herself. She wanted to ask Natalie and Hubble to stop yelling at each other, but yelling seemed to be the only way to communicate over the sirens.

Natalie waved at the gymnasium, with its alarms still blaring. All the witches on hand—staff and chaperones included—circled the building, chanting and recasting spells of protection. "So what did you plan for the final act, director? A dragon to show up and burn the school down?"

"They were supposed to live happily ever after," Hubble snapped back at her. "The rip in space that pulled Tinker through, the explosion—that was all the Goblin King's doing."

The Goblin King. Bellamy blinked. It wasn't her fault?

"Are you kidding me?" Natalie snapped. "He just magically reached in and yanked Tinker out of Harmswood like that?"

"The Goblin King has a ton of magic at his disposal," explained Hubble. "Goblin City sits on a hotspot of crossing ley lines. The goblins have been using it as a natural source of energy for as long as anyone can remember."

"I didn't mean 'where did the magic come from,'" said

Natalie. "I meant the part where an outside force managed to pluck a student right out of the gym of a secret school full of extremely powerful paranormals. I didn't know such a thing was possible."

"It's not supposed to be." Professor Blake's voice reached them over the howling alarms. "Harmswood has layers of spells in place to protect from such an event."

The Head Witch of Harmswood accompanied Kwasi and Kai—and what appeared to be most of the rest of the school —to Bellamy's resting place. Her fellow students looked none the worse for wear, beyond confused expressions and a coat of glitter from the snow globe's explosion.

Kai sat down on the stone wall and put an arm around Bellamy. Finn and Owen stood on either side of them, ever the guardsmen. Safe now, Bellamy turned her head into Kai's shoulder…and somewhere, a dam broke. All the sadness that had been building inside her burst forth in an uncontrollable wave. She tried her best to stifle the sobs, but she couldn't stop the tears.

"Ohmigosh, Bell. You're freezing." Bellamy felt additional pressure where Kai was holding her. Warm magic seeped into her skin, relaxing her muscles and thawing her bones. Having a Fury as a best friend was a definite perk for anyone in danger of hypothermia.

"A spell like the one we just witnessed requires massive amounts of energy," said Professor Blake. "It can leach that energy—often heat—from its immediate surroundings. I suppose we should be thankful it wasn't worse."

Now that she was warming up, Bellamy calmed down. She found the presence of mind to consider how the situation could have been worse. Instead of heat, that massive spell could have taken her life. Or Tinker's. Or someone else's. Multiple someones.

This time when she shuddered, it wasn't from the cold.

"Now, now. There's nothing that a nice, hot cup of tea can't fix." Mamori Zuru, Dean of Harmswood, waddled up to Professor Blake. He was a short, doddering old man, with flyaway hair on his balding head and a great round belly. Bellamy had always felt a special kinship with Dean Zuru. He was undoubtedly one of the most powerful people in Nocturne Falls, but he typically solved most of Harmswood's day to day problems with a pleasant demeanor and a drink from his never-empty teapot.

Bellamy's body gave one last shiver. A soothing cup of tea sounded really nice right about now.

"Can we do something about the...?" Dean Zuru pointed to his ear and waved his arm about in the air.

"All we need is your authorization," Professor Blake said patiently.

"Yes. Of course." The dean held his hand in the air, palm flat, and closed his eyes. Within a few seconds the alarms stopped. Everyone except Bellamy breathed a collective sigh of relief.

"Are you all right, my dear?" Professor Blake asked Bellamy.

Thanks to Kai, Bellamy at least felt well enough to answer that dreaded question. "I will be," she said. She might have been lying. She wasn't sure. "What about Tinker?"

"The Goblin King will be taken to task for his actions," Professor Blake said sharply. "One does not remove students willy-nilly from this Academy! There are proper sign-out procedures that every guardian is expected to follow."

But the dean was shaking his head. "I'm afraid we will have to let this one slide, Professor."

"Excuse me?" said Professor Blake.

"Excuse me?" Natalie echoed.

"The Harmswood Handbook does include a clause

wherein a parent or guardian may withdraw a student, unannounced, in the event of an emergency."

"Yes, but—someone could have been hurt! Never mind the disruption of this week's classes and the last remaining midterm exams...couldn't the goblins have waited until winter break like everyone else?"

Dean Zuru continued as if he hadn't noticed Professor Blake's interruption. "It seems that there were several previous missives from the Goblin King requesting Mr. Tinkerton's presence, but they all went astray."

Bellamy's gaze met Hubble's, but he quickly looked away. No one else seemed to notice their brief exchange.

"A note got to you, apparently," Professor Blake said.

"One arrived earlier today," replied the dean. "I underestimated the impatience of the sender, thinking it would be safe to send Mr. Tinkerton on his way first thing in the morning. Apparently, it was not. The fault here, I'm afraid, is mine. I will make the appropriate apologies."

Bellamy wanted to yell and scream and cry. She wanted to run away and hide, but she had promised Kai that she would stay, no matter what. As it was, she only had enough energy to shake her head slightly. None of this was anyone's fault. It was a terrible situation, and sometimes terrible situations just happened. No one was to blame. Not her. Not Dean Zuru. Not even the Goblin King.

The only question now was: Where did they go from here?

Bellamy wasn't exactly sure of the answer. But she didn't want to go on without Tinker.

Professor Blake's lips became a thin line of dissatisfaction. She clapped her hands three times and addressed the crowd. "I'm afraid the dance is over, children. Boarding students, please return to your rooms. Local students, if you need assistance with transportation, please see Professor Van Zant."

The dean reached up and placed a gnarled hand on Professor Blake's considerably taller shoulder. "Give our young people a moment, Theodosia. No need to rush. They've been through a lot tonight."

"We all have," muttered Professor Blake. She let the dean lead her back through the crowd, toward the administrative wing. Where, presumably, they would share a nice, calming cup of tea.

Bellamy expected the rest of the students to disappear with the professors...but none of them did.

"They're not going to do anything," Natalie said in the teachers' wake. "They're really not going to do anything."

"Are you surprised?" asked Sam.

"I suppose not, but..." Natalie growled at the sky in frustration.

"My parents are going to freak when they find out about this," said one of the fae girls.

"Mine won't," said one of the gargoyles.

"At least you have parents," Owen added with great condescension.

"Don't worry," said Kai. "Dean Zuru will smooth things over with all the teachers and parents. It's what he does best."

"Great," spat Hubble. "But Tinker will still be gone."

"Boo hoo." The crowd parted to reveal Heather Hayden, fellow cheerleader and the most popular—and meanest—girl at Harmswood. Even the snow seemed too frightened to land on her black silk dress. "Tinker's daddy stole him away so he could go be a king. My heart weeps for him."

"Yeah," said one of Heather's cronies.

"Boo hoo," repeated the other.

Why was Heather even still here? Bellamy figured she and her fellow Gothwitches would have been the first to leave.

"Goblins don't have fathers," said Maya. "Or mothers. Or sisters. Don't you know anything about goblins?"

"I try not to," sneered Heather.

"They're called Lost Boys because they don't have families," said Finn. "Some of us know a little something about that."

"Oh, really, Lone Wolf? Was this a story you heard from your *cousin*?" Heather asked with complete insensitivity. Finn's cousins did live in the Falls, but he'd only come to town because his original wolf-shifter pack had beaten him and left him for dead.

Finn stood up with a growl and bared his teeth at the witch. It wasn't Kai who held him back—of all people, it was Owen. "It's not worth it, mate."

"Tinker has no desire to be in Goblin City," said Hubble. "Trust me."

"He's going to be a *king*," Heather argued. "Who wouldn't want to be king?"

"Yeah," said the first Gothwitch.

"All hail King Tinker," said the other.

Hubble threw his mask and hat on the ground and stomped up to Heather and her cronies. No one held him back. "Have you ever been to Goblin City? Any of you?"

No one answered. Because no one had. As a child, Bellamy had heard stories from her parents, fairy tales from distant lands, but she could never be sure which parts were true.

"Goblin City is a trash pile. Kobolds are hoarders by nature, and even we make fun of the goblins. Their population is made up of a bunch of ex-human freak kids no one wanted. The Lost Boys become thieves and ne'er-do-wells who live hard and die young. Their 'city' is a dilapidated maze, and their vaults are full of worthless garbage."

Now that he had everyone's attention, Hubble hopped up

on the stone wall beside Bellamy and Kai. "Do any of you remember the last time there was a goblin at Harmswood? No. Because there hasn't been one. Tinker got here on a scholarship because he was smart. *Is* smart. At Harmswood, he had an opportunity to do something useful with his life. He had the chance to be a productive member of society. Now he gets to be King of Nothing. Yeah. Lucky him."

Heather, never one to admit defeat, crossed her arms over her chest. "Fine. Bellamy, what do *you* want to do?"

"I agree," said Lian. "This is all up to Bellamy."

"Whatever you need us to do, Bellamy," said Ace. His gargoyle brethren fanned out behind him, like soldiers. "Just say the word."

For the second time that night Bellamy was dumbstruck. She had sat there, coming out of her shock, watching this drama unfold, and only now did she realize why Heather was still in the courtyard. Why they all were.

They were there for her.

The cheerleading squad. The sports teams. The masquerade decorating committee. The parade planners. The festival staffers. Every kid in her classes. Every girl on her floor. Every werewolf, witch, and gargoyle she'd ever made a drink for at The Hallowed Bean.

Bellamy clasped her hands together and beamed with pride. Her circle of friends was so much bigger than Kai and Maya and Tinker and Owen and Finn. It encompassed this whole courtyard. The whole school. This was her tribe. Her true family. Her *Harmswood* family.

"What do you want to do, Bellamy?" Kai asked softly.

"I want to find a way," she answered tentatively.

"A way to do what?" asked Sam.

Bellamy knew her words wouldn't be as eloquent as Hubble's, but she got them out anyway. "Maybe Tinker and I have a future together, maybe we don't, but I have to find out. If Tinker wants to come back to Harmswood, I want to find a way to make that possible."

"Being king—no matter what he's king of—comes with responsibilities," said Kwasi. The son of a god knew a thing or two about that kind of responsibility.

Hubble, still perched on the stone wall, gave Kwasi a withering look.

"He may not be in a position to return is all I'm saying," Kwasi added.

"It's a good point," said Bellamy. "If Tinker doesn't want to come back, or if it's not possible, then I just want to find a way to communicate with him in Goblin City. We lost him, but that doesn't mean he has to lose us."

Bellamy looked directly at Hubble when she said that last part; the kobold nodded in solidarity. She didn't have to wait long for her other friends to chime in.

"Yeah."

"Tinker's not getting rid of us that easily."

"His stupid jokes actually made Physics bearable."

"If I can't cheat off his paper, how else am I going to pass Calculus?"

"Our early morning pick-up games won't be the same without him."

"He still owes me ten bucks," Sam added with a wink.

"Let's do it," said Hubble.

Bellamy's smile grew even brighter. Tinker constantly told her that nobody at Harmswood cared about him—she wished he could see this show of support right now. They might not have said so out loud, but the students here loved Tinker just as much as they loved Bellamy. He was, for better or worse, an essential part of their world.

"I know what we have to do." Bellamy sat up straight; Kai's hands fell away from her shoulders. "We're going to get him back."

"When you say 'we,'" said Kai, "who do you mean exactly?"

"I can hold my own in a fight," said Finn. "As can any of the were-shifters." Every are in the crowd added their agreements.

"And the gargoyles," said Ace. "We've got strength."

"And we've got power," Maya said, indicating herself, Kai, and even Heather.

Kwasi chimed in. "I've got a few tricks up my sleeve," he said with a twinkle in his dark eyes.

"With all due respect," Hubble announced to the crowd, "she means me."

"And me," Sam and Natalie said in unison.

"They're right," said Bellamy. "Hubble and Sam and Natalie are exactly who I had in mind." For one thing, by the time they made a plan, most of these folks would have departed for winter break. Hubble, Sam and Natalie's families could only afford to bring them home for the summer.

There was silence for a moment as the crowd considered Bellamy's decision.

"I get why Hubble should go, since he knows more about goblins than any of us," Finn said to Bellamy. "But—no offense, guys— wouldn't it make more sense for someone like Owen or me to come with you?"

Owen puffed out his chest. "I do happen to be brilliant at spy work."

"Sam and Natalie are uniquely qualified for this job," said Hubble. "They have been questing in dungeons with Tinker and me since they arrived at Harmswood."

"You mean that game you guys play," sneered Heather. "Not *actual* dungeons."

"Does it matter?" Hubble asked. "Training is mental as well as physical. We aren't just a team, we're a well-oiled machine. Each of us knows how the other thinks. We can communicate without speaking. We can anticipate each other's moves and play to our strengths. We can get to Tinker—and get him out—in the fastest, most efficient way possible."

"He's right," said Sam. The gargoyles and weres were also nodding—they knew about teams and packs.

"We can do it," said Natalie. In her blood red outfit, with that impressive skull headdress, she looked ready to lead a raiding party. No one was about to contradict her.

"But we'll still need everyone's help to prepare," Bellamy told her friends. "We'll meet up with each of you separately as our plan unfolds. In the meantime, we should get some rest. Thank y'all so very, very much. I don't know what I'd do without you."

Kai hugged her. "We love you, Bell."

"I'm so sorry this happened," said Finn.

"We'll make those dirty goblins pay for what they've done," said Owen.

Maya squeezed her hand. "Anything you need."

One by one, the rest of the student body bid their personal farewells to Bellamy. Each kind word seemed to heal a piece of her broken heart. *Let your friends lift you up for a change*, Kai had told her. And so they had.

"Come on," Lian said, when there were only a handful of people left in the courtyard. "Natalie and I will walk you back to the room."

Bellamy nodded. Despite her instructions for everyone to go to bed, there was no way she'd be getting any sleep tonight. But she had the seed of a plan now, and enough hope to see her through its execution.

As they crossed the quiet, empty courtyard, the snow began to fall again.

"Totally off the subject," Bellamy said to her friends, "but do either of you have any idea what happened to my sister?"

8

Tinker opened his eyes…and then slammed them shut again.

He didn't want to be awake. He didn't want this life to be the real one.

He didn't remember much of the night before. His non-traditional arrival in the Goblin City had left him spellsick. Unable to stand or speak, Tinker remembered succumbing to the blackness again sometime in the middle of Maker Deng's magnanimous greeting.

He didn't remember dreaming, which was a shame. He would have liked to have been in that snow globe one last time. In Bellamy's arms. In that perfect moment full of golden hair and glitter and laughter and hope and the possibility of a future together.

Theirs was a love worth giving up a kingdom for.

But recalling those moments wouldn't help anyone right now. Tinker shoved the image of his beloved fairy into a mental vault and locked her there. He needed to show no emotion the next time he met with the Goblin King. Tinker's feelings would do nothing but give Maker the upper hand.

Think about something else.

Tinker slowly rose to a sitting position. Every bit of his body was sore, from the tips of his toes to the top of his head. He'd been moved to a room in the keep, he guessed. Some sort of servant quarters, judging by the considerable lack of "treasures" junking up the walls. It might have also been a guest room. The Lost Boys took over this castle and occupied its grounds hundreds of years ago, but goblins had neither guests nor servants, so the majority of the keep went unused.

Both the bed and room were bigger than his dorm at Harmswood. Was this to be his chamber now? Like his first year at school, he didn't feel like he belonged in it. It was too empty.

And there was no Hubble.

One tall goblin and one short kobold with very few resources between them still managed to accumulate a lot of stuff. And it had been great stuff. Everything that Tinker and Hubble had amassed over the years had a memory attached to it—the sum of their hoard could retell their lives. As a collection it would have been worthless in the eyes of their fancy-pants schoolmates, but each item meant something to *them*. Like a 3D scrapbook.

Everything in Goblin City had been obtained because it held some perceived value to someone else, somewhere else. In Tinker's eyes, if an object didn't have personal purpose or meaning—be it a diamond or a gum wrapper—it was junk.

Certainly not an opinion shared by the reigning Goblin King.

The image of Bellamy's makeshift necklace popped into Tinker's mind unbidden, its flash of dull silver dangling from a blue ribbon. So much faith and love embodied in one heart-shaped piece of tin. He was a fool for ever calling it garbage.

One goblin's trash is another fairy's treasure.

Oh, Bellamy…

Think about something else.

His clothes had been changed, he noticed. The fancy costume was gone, replaced by a threadbare shirt and loose trousers that were too short for his frame. It was for the best. Seeing those ruffles again would have been too painful, for many reasons.

Sunlight crept in through a crack in the curtains and streaked across Tinker's bed. There was glitter on his pillow. He left it there.

There was a cursory knock on the door before Retcher entered with a tray of food. The tray had once been a shield, stolen from some ancient warrior or rescued from some foreign battlefield. Judging by the decadent smell, the food it bore was Aberdeen's apple cake: a treat Tinker only ever had on special occasions, but a breakfast fit for a prince. There was fresh coffee, too. The bittersweet odor was like a punch in the gut.

If he couldn't get back to Nocturne Falls, there would be no more meetings to play Dungeons and Dragons at the Bean. Bellamy would never make coffee for him again.

Bellamy…

Think about something else.

Retcher looked tired.

"Let me take that, old man." Tinker moved the tray to his bed and pulled up a chair. "Rest your weary bones."

"Not long ago I would have taken you over my knee for that remark," said Retcher. "But I'm afraid these weary bones have only gotten wearier. And you're a prince now."

"I will always be that ragamuffin baby you rescued from the trash heap," said Tinker. But as much as he would have enjoyed a convivial visit with Retcher, he wanted to get the lay of the land. "Have you come to deliver me to the king?"

"All in good time," Retcher said as he settled into the chair with a grunt. "In anticipation of his upcoming retirement, King Maker has started sleeping in. He refuses to make any appointments before midday."

"Midday? What time is it now?" Tinker gave Retcher the side-eye. "After all the king went through to bring me back to the city, he'd rather sleep instead of see me?"

"Of course. Now that you're back, the rest comes easier."

It made a bizarre sort of sense, when very little in the last few weeks had made any sense at all. "Retcher, what's really going on? You and I both know I have no business being anywhere near the king's throne."

"Is that why you ignored all his requests to come home?"

"Mostly," said Tinker. Which was mostly the truth. Maker did have a tendency to change his mind at the drop of a hat… but apparently not after dropping a Mantle of Majesty.

Retcher cleared his overly-phlegmy throat. "Well, I for one am glad you're back."

"Where's Quin?" If Tinker was going to put the original heir to the throne back in his rightful place, he needed to know where to begin.

Retcher chuckled. "Pretty Boy caught the wrong end of the Goblin King on the wrong day."

"Don't let Maker catch you calling him that," said Tinker. He and a handful of the boys had started calling Quin "Pretty Boy" in secret. The name never should have caught on, but it was just too fitting.

Quin had always been the perfect specimen of goblin-hood: strong and handsome, and he knew it. But then, the Mantle of Majesty had been bestowed upon Quin at a very young age. It never occurred to Tinker to put two and two together. He and all his goblin brothers just assumed Quin had won the genetic lottery, while the rest of them grew greener and wartier as the years went on.

"Quin's ego was always going to be his downfall," said

Tinker. "It was only a matter of time. But what happened that pushed Maker so far over the edge?"

Retcher cracked his thick, wart-covered knuckles. "Maker found out that Quin was keeping a special squad, separate from the king's own goblin gangs."

"Quin organized his own unit? What did he have them doing?"

"His bidding, mostly." The end of the statement was lost in a raspy cough. "You gonna drink that?"

Tinker didn't like the sound of that cough. His gaze dropped to the cooling mug of coffee on the tray beside him; he'd completely forgotten it was there. "You want it? It's all yours. And…wait, is that *fresh* cream?" He couldn't remember the last time Goblin City had seen fresh dairy products of any sort.

Retcher dumped a generous splash of said cream into the mug. "You know how Pickafur's always been good with animals…"

"Yeah," said Tinker.

"Aberdeen convinced Maker to steal him a cow. So we did."

Tinker raised an eyebrow. Over the years, Tinker and Retcher had had many discussions about the merits of teaching the Lost Boys how to legitimately fend for themselves, as opposed to stealing everything they needed to survive. It wasn't a concept Maker had ever been on board with. Goblins had always been the thieving pirates of the paranormal world, and the Goblin King didn't see any reason to completely overhaul his people's way of life.

"*Aberdeen* convinced the king?"

Retcher shrugged and scratched his oversized nose. "I may have had some small say in it, but the final decision was Maker's alone. And thank goodness. The quality of the apple cake has gone up considerably. Good enough that if you don't eat yours up right quick, I'll happily polish it off for you."

Tinker was about to offer Retcher the cake, but his stomach growled in protest.

Retcher pointed at the tray. "Eat! You'll not get out of this crown prince business by dying of starvation. I won't let you."

Did Retcher suspect Tinker's plan to "get out of this crown prince business" at the first opportunity? Not that he had a plan yet—there hadn't been time to make one. But soon...

Reluctantly, Tinker took a bite of the apple cake. Aberdeen had outdone himself. It was both flaky and moist in the most delicious way. The chunks of apple were soft and sweet. He would have thought changing the recipe in any way was blasphemy, but Aberdeen had gone and made something exquisite. And yet, the flavor still reminded Tinker of autumn, and home.

Home.

He had never hated being home before. But then, Goblin City had never felt like a prison before.

A single tear, sponsored by all the memories he'd tried to lock away, managed to escape. Tinker let it fall.

Retcher nodded. "Told you it was good."

Tinker concentrated on chewing.

With a groan, his mentor lifted himself up from the chair and swatted at some of the hair that fell into his face. "Come on. Grab the tray. You can thank Aberdeen yourself. I know how much he loves to see you. You always were his favorite."

Tinker took up the shield and followed Retcher—still leisurely sipping his coffee—out the door. They passed by a badly-scarred chest of drawers, on top of which sat the Mantle of Malice and the goblin mask that Sam and Natalie had made him.

Tinker ignored them both.

He nodded to the two guards stationed outside his room —they stood at attention in their armor adorned with colorful strips cut from soda cans. Once on the street, they passed a group of goblins betting on a game of Elf Bones: a modified version of Jacks. Only this bunch was playing with a rubber ball and handfuls of raw emeralds. As they approached the keep's separate kitchen, Tinker and Retcher were almost tackled by Fork and Willie, who sped past them.

"Watch it, goonies!" Tinker managed to catch Retcher before he toppled over, dropping the makeshift tray in the process. The plate and saucer both slipped off and shattered on the stone.

"Hooray!" A chorus of voices from inside the kitchen cheered at the sound of breaking porcelain.

"Who's out there bringing good luck to my doorstep today?" Aberdeen cried out.

"Our prodigal son has returned," Retcher announced as Tinker stopped to pick up the shards. The sound of breaking glass might have been good luck in their culture, but most goblins ran around barefoot—as he and Retcher currently were. It would have been irresponsible to leave the mess. Especially right outside Aberdeen's workplace.

"Ranulf! Is he back, finally?" Aberdeen had always taken great pleasure in calling Tinker by his given birth name. He was one of the rare Lost Boys who actually had one; it had been stitched into the blanket Retcher had found him swaddled in.

"I'm back, whether I want to be or not," Tinker said dolefully.

Aberdeen raised his arms in the air and waved his hands about wildly. "Come here, kiddo. Let me see you! It's been too long."

The goblin chef was almost as dramatic as Hubble. "It's

only been a couple of months," Tinker said, but he obligingly walked over and bent his face down for inspection. Aberdeen's strong fingers flew across Tinker's face: the bridge of his nose, the furrow of his brow, the lines of his cheekbones and jaw.

"Handsome as ever!" Aberdeen pulled him into an enthusiastic embrace. "And so much bigger since the summer. Francis! William! Stop gobbling up all my berries and fetch our growing boy another slice of cake."

Refusing food from Aberdeen was about as futile as refusing Retcher, so Tinker focused on something else. "Francis?" he asked.

"Ain't my name to you, *Ranulf*," Fork spat. "Only Aberdeen gets to call me that."

"I needed an assistant, and we discovered that randomly yelling 'Fork' in a kitchen confuses things rather quickly," said Aberdeen.

"I didn't know either of you had an interest in cooking," Tinker said to the twins.

"Got me an interest in food," said Fork. "Soos-chefs get to taste everything."

"And eat all the failures," Willie added cheerfully.

"Francis and William have become surprisingly invaluable to me," said Aberdeen. "I believe they have a true aptitude for the culinary arts."

At the moment, the twins showed an aptitude for throwing overripe berries at each other. Aberdeen picked up the wooden spoon beside him and banged it against the table. "Boys! What have we learned?"

Fork and Willie immediately stopped their shenanigans and stood at attention. "Not to waste food," Fork said sheepishly.

"And never to rearrange the spice cabinet," said Willie. "Or anything else."

Tinker had done his own stint as Aberdeen's assistant many summers ago. For the kitchen to function around the blind chef, everything needed to be kept in a very specific, orderly fashion. Tinker also knew Aberdeen's tricks when it came to punishing mischievous, hungry young boys.

"There was an unfortunate hot pepper incident a few weeks back," Aberdeen said with mock concern, "but everything's ship shape now. Right, boys?"

"Yes, chef!"

Aberdeen smiled at the twins' response, almost as if he could see their salute. Fork began to clean up the berry mess —mostly with his tongue—while Willie wrapped up another piece of apple cake in paper and delivered it to Tinker. It was still warm.

"Thank you again for the apple cake," Tinker told Aberdeen. "It's my favorite part about being back in the city. And you've done wonders with the new recipe."

"Thank Pickafur for that," said the chef. "Though I do wish he'd stay out of my kitchen. Every time he tromps through in those disgusting boots, the whole place reeks of cows and chickens. My tastebuds are completely useless until it airs out."

"Chickens?" asked Tinker.

"We have a whole coop now!" Fork announced.

"Eggs for days," said Willie.

"Such an abundance that today we're trying our hands at berry soufflé," said Aberdeen. "Wish us luck!"

"Better yet, wish us lots and lots of failures," said Willie.

Tinker laughed. He embraced Aberdeen and kissed the chef heartily on the cheek. "Best of luck, chef. I look forward to sampling your final product."

"It will be an honor, my prince," Aberdeen replied solemnly.

Tinker was glad that Aberdeen could not see how much

he hated being called "prince." Thankfully, if Retcher noticed Tinker's reaction, he did not say anything. Ignoring Aberdeen's sentimentality, Fork and Willie began regaling Retcher with stories they'd heard about legendary soufflés.

"I voted for you," Aberdeen whispered into Tinker's ear. "Just so you know."

Tinker blinked several times in rapid succession. "I'm sorry, what? You voted for *what?*"

"For you to be king," the chef said, as if the Lost Boys coming together to decide anything wasn't a monumentally rare event. "Maker announced that he was dropping Quin in a deep dark hole as punishment for something. He didn't care to explain. Retcher didn't openly oppose the king's decision, but he pointed out that Maker wouldn't be able to leave Goblin City as he'd planned, because we wouldn't have a king. So we picked one, right then and there."

Tinker could hardly believe his ears. "You. All of you?"

"Yes," said Aberdeen. "As far as I could tell. Every goblin who was there, anyway. It was a fairly unanimous decision."

"But...why me?"

Aberdeen gave him a smirk. "Because you make things better, my dear boy. Having you home is a joyous occasion for us all."

Tinker pinched the bridge of his nose as the chef's explanation sank in. Tinker could be mad at Maker all he wanted for pulling him out of Harmswood right when the pieces of his life finally started coming together...but he couldn't be mad at his goblin brothers.

The Lost Boys needed him in the Goblin City. They *wanted* him there.

Emotions overwhelmed Tinker, but he forced himself not to let them show. He wasn't even sure how he would have expressed them if he did. The image of Bellamy's angelic smile flashed in his mind.

He knew exactly what Bellamy would say about this. She'd tell him that she loved him…right before she reminded him of the importance of family and his responsibility to his people. She'd never allow him to leave Goblin City without a king to lead it.

Oh, Bellamy.

Tinker knew he should think about something else, but he couldn't. This was too important.

When they were far enough away from the kitchen, Retcher turned to Tinker. "We don't have to go straight to Maker's quarters if you don't want." He paused, and then went on. "If you need more time to think of a way to get out of this, I can find some more errands for us to run."

Tinker almost smiled at that. His mentor knew him all too well. But deep in the pit of his stomach, Tinker felt like he was going to be sick again.

"Let's just get this over with."

"Are you going to throw your apple cake in Maker's face before you refuse him?" Retcher's brow furrowed. He coughed again and cleared his throat. "I don't mind, whatever you decide to do. I just want to be prepared."

Tinker had almost forgotten the carefully wrapped cake he held in his hand. "No. None of that."

"So what do you plan to do when he hands you his crown?"

Tinker took a deep breath. "I'm going to accept it."

9

Hubble, ever the director at heart, took point on organizing the whole adventure, from escaping Harmswood to Tinker's (hopeful) recovery. Natalie played devil's advocate, skillfully poking as many holes in the plan as she could so that Hubble could preemptively address them. Amiable Sam quietly gathered information and collected allies from all over the school.

Bellamy brought the coffee.

When the fairy and the kobold butted heads over Bellamy's lack of participation, Hubble pointed out that she was too visible. Bellamy had always been Harmswood's constant light of cheerful optimism. Now, more than ever, everyone was watching her. Teachers were concerned about Bellamy's physical and emotional well-being in the wake of the masquerade. The students waited with bated breath, knowing that something big was going to happen without knowing when.

"You're the perfect distraction," said Hubble. "The absolute best thing you can do right now is nothing at all."

As frustrating as it was, Bellamy knew Hubble was right. Reluctantly, she'd allowed him to take the lead.

Meanwhile, she carried on the best she could. She threw herself into the Frozen in Fear Festival and helped out wherever needed. She studied like mad for every midterm, not that she could recall a word of the tests once she'd taken them.

Her answer to the refraction question on her Physics exam had been stained with silent tears.

Bellamy smiled and laughed and cheered with great fervor. She bid farewell to the friends who left for winter break. If it was more difficult for her to do those things than ever before, no one noticed. Bellamy went on lifting everyone's spirits except her own, distracting herself with activities that in turn distracted everyone else from the plans her crew was making on the sly.

Inside, Bellamy counted down the moments until she could see Tinker again.

They met in Hubble's room the day of their escape. It was easier to meet there—girls were mostly allowed to come and go as they pleased in the boys' wing during daylight hours, but the rules were much stricter the other way around. Some of the female students turned into creatures that ate men after midnight.

"I keep waiting for Hubble to straighten up," Bellamy said to Natalie as she set the Hallowed Bean coffee carrier on the table. "It still looks like Tinker just stepped out, doesn't it? I keep feeling like he's going to walk back through that door any minute. And then he doesn't, and it hurts all over again."

"He will." Natalie squeezed Bellamy's hand. "Soon. We're going make sure of it."

But it was Sam who walked in through the door instead, his arms laden with yards of gray-green fabric.

"It's about time, slow-poke," growled Hubble.

Natalie smacked the kobold on the arm. "Hey! I'm the only one who's allowed to verbally abuse my brother in that fashion." She pointed to the Hallowed Bean cups. "Drink up. Maybe it will make you less of a grouch."

Hubble gave Natalie a growl that would have made a feral wolf proud. Until then, Bellamy had not realized just how many of Hubble's teeth were pointed. Perhaps the ancient fairy tales about rogue bands of bloodthirsty kobolds weren't that far off after all. "We have to toast Tinker first," he said through those teeth.

"Like we do at the beginning of every meeting," said Sam. "It's tradition."

"And necessary today, more than ever. Here, hand me that cup back real quick." Bellamy popped the lids on all of the drinks and proceeded to give each one a healthy dose of fairy dust. "For good luck."

"Is this enough to make me fly?" Hubble asked hopefully.

"Not quite," Bellamy said with a smile.

"I didn't think your own fairy dust affected you," said Sam.

"It won't hurt. Besides, your good luck is my good luck." Bellamy lifted her own cup. "For one…"

"…for all," they answered, and then sipped.

"I feel like this occasion calls for drinks we should guzzle," said Hubble. "This coffee is too hot."

"But amazing," Sam said with a healthy swig. "Thanks, Bell."

"You're welcome," the fairy said with a smile. "And that's not all I've brought you."

From the magic pocket in her skirt, Bellamy pulled the three extra pieces of tin from the goblins' Mantle of Majesty.

"Four of these fell on the day the Lost Boys made Tinker their heir. Kai fixed them for me. It just seemed…important…for us to wear these on our quest." The minute the explanation left her lips, it sounded ridiculous. "But of course, you don't have to if you don't—"

Natalie snatched one of the bits out of Bellamy's hand. "Girl, stop yammering and pass them around already. You got another piece of ribbon?"

Bellamy hadn't removed her own necklace since Tinker's disappearance—the blue ribbon was beginning to fade, but she didn't care. Some superstitious part of her thought that the longer she wore it, the better the chance would be for Tinker's return. "I brought some leather to use, if y'all have somethin' to cut it with."

"Of course," said Hubble.

"Here. Tie mine on." Natalie turned her back to Bellamy as Hubble hopped up to fetch the scissors.

Sam flipped his own piece of tin between his fingers. "Tinker would have wanted us to have these. Thank you, Bellamy."

"This officially makes us King's Men," said Hubble.

"Almost-king," Sam clarified.

"Rogue Prince," said Natalie.

Bellamy snipped the piece of leather dangling from Natalie's back and threaded it through Sam's piece of tin. "Rogue Prince. I like that."

"Says the princess," Hubble muttered.

"I'm not sure I deserve that," she said. Of all the ways Bellamy imagined this plan could play out, and all the ways she'd imagined herself back by Tinker's side, she had never considered herself a princess.

"Why not?" asked the kobold. "Our entire plan hinges around you."

"You're our ace in the hole," Sam said as he emptied his cup.

"Really?" asked Bellamy. "I thought y'all were just bringin' me along for the coffee."

"Are you kidding?" Hubble fidgeted as Bellamy tied the last piece of tin around his neck. "In a city full of goblins, you're a weapon of mass destruction."

Bellamy's fingers stilled on the knot. She hadn't considered that either. "I don't want to hurt anyone."

Hubble shrugged. "Neither do we. But the threat alone is power."

"You gotta wonder why no fairy ever walked into Goblin City and took it over before this," said Sam.

"There's nothing there a fairy would want," said Hubble. "The king of the trash pile is typically safe in his domain."

Bellamy didn't find Hubble's comment particularly amusing, but Sam laughed so hard at the joke that he snorted.

"Job security, am I right?" Hubble added with a wiggle of his silver eyebrows.

Sam doubled over with giggles.

Natalie eyed her brother before turning to Bellamy. "You meant coffee and hot chocolate, right?"

"Beg pardon?"

"When you said 'I'll bring coffee,' please tell me you meant three coffees and one hot chocolate. For Sam."

Bellamy's eyes widened. "Sam said he wanted coffee this time, to fortify himself for our big adventure. He said it would be fine since the full moon passed a few days ago."

Natalie sighed. "Never believe anything my brother says. Especially when he wants something."

Bellamy's heart sank. "Did I just kill the plan?"

"No," said Natalie. "We can still execute the plan. It's just going to be a little more...challenging. BOYS!" Natalie pounded her fist on the coffee table to get their attention. "Focus, please. Let's go over this one last time."

"Me first! Me first!" Sam said excitedly. "I will go down in approximately five-point-three minutes to work my volunteer shift in the library."

"Is one of the gargoyles down there now?" Bellamy asked.

"Yeah," said Sam. "It's Ace. We're good."

"The rest of us will enter the library in fifteen minute intervals, so as not to raise suspicion," said Hubble. "I'll bring the cloaks—no sense in putting them on until we're ready to cross through the mirror."

"And if you're caught with a bag full of costumes, no one will think anything of it," said Natalie. "I'll bring the pack with the supplies."

"I wanna bring the snacks!" Sam said adamantly.

Bellamy winced. She had a sinking feeling that this over-excited version of Sam was going to blow their cover before they even got to the traveling mirror, and it would be all her fault.

"Fine," said Natalie. "We will rendezvous in the stacks at the top of the hour. But where?"

"Not the 900s," said Hubble. "Too many ghosts hang around biographies. I don't want them giving us away."

"The 300s then," said Natalie. "Costumes and customs."

"That should be safe enough," said Hubble. "If there's anyone else in the library at that time, Ace can distract them."

"I will steal the key to the vault!" Sam announced.

"Yes, Master Thief," Natalie said calmly. "Just make sure you're a little quieter than you are right now."

"I will be as quiet as a mouse!" Sam whisper-yelled.

"At which point, we will all slip into the vault and hop through the mirror and no one will be any the wiser," said Hubble.

"And what if we get caught?" Bellamy couldn't help but ask.

Those silver eyebrows raised mischievously. "We improvise. Now, soldier, hop to it!"

"Yes, sir!" Sam saluted Hubble, snapped up the pack that

was filled with food and first-aid supplies, and fled down the hall at breakneck speed.

"Gods help us all," Natalie said after her brother.

Fifteen minutes seemed to take forever. Bellamy was the first to go down to the library, down and down into the darkest parts of the school.

The Harmswood library housed thousands of books on every subject imaginable; the rows of shelves seemed to go on forever. The air was thick with the smell of old books and older spells. Some of the books sat docilely on their shelves. Some had to be chained in place. Some faded in and out of existence, depending on the time of day, the time of year, or just the lighting.

Outside the main stacks there were several rooms in the library for arcane texts, one room devoted entirely to the history of Harmswood, and the vault. In that vault, surrounded by stone and spells and accessible only by a key held by the librarian, were some of the most powerful and chaotic objects the world had ever seen...including a magic traveling mirror.

Bellamy knew of the mirror's existence because there was a legend about an instance where it was used—a student whose home was halfway around the world had a family member suddenly taken ill. Or taken prisoner. Or released from a thousand-year-old spell. There were many versions of the story, but one detail always remained the same: the traveling mirror.

"Hello, Bellamy!"

She gave Ace and the still-very-loud Sam a cursory wave as she entered the library, and then began to wander through the stacks.

The clock on the wall ticked like molasses.

Bellamy made her way over to the section full of costumes from around the world...this world, and others.

Her eyes slid to the fairy tale and folklore books across the aisle. A colorful spine caught her eye. She took the book off the shelf, cracked it open, and immediately felt at ease. All the stories shelved here were like her comfort food. If she lost track of time—which she sincerely hoped she did—Hubble and Natalie were sure to find her.

But the next person that appeared in the aisle was neither Hubble nor Natalie. It was Professor Blake.

Oh, nasty word.

"Missing home?" Professor Blake said with a nod to the massive collections of fairy tales on either side of them.

"Always," Bellamy answered. Which was true, but right now she was missing a lot more than just her family back in South Carolina.

"My heart goes out to those of you who can't return home for every school break."

"It's all right," said Bellamy. "I enjoy the quiet."

Her heart began to pound. Getting detained by the Head Witch wasn't in their plan. *Tinker, we're on our way. Don't give up...*

"I am aware that your family originally came from a world beyond ours," said the Professor. "In a time beyond our own. Do you find that the fairy stories we tell here are very different from the ones you were raised on?"

It was an odd topic of conversation, to be sure. But Bellamy liked Professor Blake, so she humored her. "Some are, yes. Which stands to reason, as there are so many versions of the same tales in this world alone."

"But the same tropes still resonate, do they not?" the professor asked. "The good sister and bad sister, the young man seeking his fortune, the clever servant..."

The ill-fated lovers, Bellamy thought but did not say. "Yes, we have similar themes in our tales."

"My favorites were always the fairy beggars," said Professor Blake.

"You mean the beggars who turned out to be fairies in disguise?" Bellamy smiled. "I like to imagine that there really are fairies out there who spend their whole lives waitin' around to help people, always encouragin' them to be kind and generous and pure of heart. Not that they'd ever exist in real life. But it's nice to think about."

"Oh, I don't know," mused the professor. "I suspect if those fairies did exist, they'd be a lot like you."

Professor Blake's kindness touched her. Bellamy tried not to dwell on the fact that she and her friends were on the verge of breaking about a thousand school rules. "Thank you, Professor."

The Head Witch slid an old, weathered tome off a high shelf. "Have faith, Bellamy. Everything will turn out all right in the end."

It will take a miracle, Bellamy thought. With her outside voice she said, "Have a good day, Professor."

"You as well, my dear." As the professor turned to go, Bellamy glanced at the clock. It wasn't quite the top of the hour yet. Where were Hubble and Natalie and Sam?

When Professor Blake reached the center aisle, her face brightened. "Dean Zuru! Just the man I wanted to see."

Bellamy lost her breath. If the dean was here, there was no way they'd be able to break into the vault, never mind escape through the mirror. She looked back down at the book in her hands, but she was freaking out too much to read. What were they going to do? This kind of thing always happened in movies—a wrench in the works at the last minute. Hubble said they should improvise. She could solve this problem. She *had* to solve this problem.

Think, Bellamy, think...

The words on the page continued to swim before her as Natalie brushed up against her shoulder.

"The dean is here," Natalie whispered between her teeth. Hubble stood on her other side.

"I know," Bellamy whispered back. "And the Head Witch!"

"What do we do?" Natalie asked.

"I'm wrackin' my brain. Hubble? Any great ideas?"

"Only one." Hubble's lids fell over his frantic blue eyes and he sighed a little. "The last ditch idea. I sacrifice myself for the team."

"No!" Natalie whispered. "I'll do it. You're the Dungeon Master. You go with Bellamy."

Bellamy didn't want to sacrifice anyone. The whole point was to track down Tinker as a team. Before she could add her opinion, Sam burst around the corner.

"I have the key!" He didn't whisper.

Hubble moved to clamp his hand over Sam's mouth, but Sam's lips already seemed glued shut. Sam's hands flew to his mouth and his eyes widened in horror.

"What the...?" Natalie started to ask, but Bellamy already knew the answer. She'd seen this very thing happen to a few students during her tenure at Harmswood. Hubble had, too, having once been on the receiving end of it.

Because no one defied Professor Blake without consequences.

Together, Bellamy and Hubble dared to peek into the center aisle. Dean Zuru had his back to them. Professor Blake was still speaking to him...but her gaze was fixed on Bellamy and Hubble. Quickly, as quick as a twitch, one eye closed and opened again.

Professor Blake had just winked at them.

Theodosia Blake: Head Witch of Harmswood and granddaughter of a Necromancer. The one witch who could make the entire student body sit down and shut up with a wave of her hand. The one woman who could end their school careers right then and there with but a word. Professor Blake...was on their side.

Hubble turned back to Sam and placed a comforting hand on his shoulder. "Relax," he said softly. "It's a spell. Just go with it."

Bellamy whispered an explanation in Natalie's ear in an effort to ease her anger. "Professor Blake is helpin' us."

Natalie's brows furrowed, but she kept her mouth closed. Sam, still frightened, nodded a bit. Then his head tilted, the hand with the key flew up before him, and he marched with a soldier's efficiency to the door of the vault. Hubble hefted his bag of cloaks and followed. Natalie lifted Sam's precious bag of snacks and did the same. Bellamy brought up the rear.

"Thank you," she mouthed to her very own benevolent fairy-in-disguise.

Professor Blake gave an almost imperceptible bob of her head before turning her full attention back to Dean Zuru.

By the time Bellamy made it into the vault, the magic mirror had already been activated, and her friends had presumably slipped through to Goblin City. She made sure to close the vault door behind her as quietly as possible, and then she jumped.

Traveling through the magic mirror was much like being swept down Nocturne Falls. A light glowed glittery and white, and then was gone. There was a crash in her eardrums like the rush of water. Instinctively, Bellamy pulled her wings in tight to her body and closed her eyes. Her clothes felt heavy and damp.

She *was* being swept away, she decided, in some sort of river. Underground, maybe, since there was no light? For all she knew, the magic mirror had dumped them straight into Goblin City's sewer system. Or perhaps just Bellamy, since she was fae—it would have been a clever goblin defense mechanism. A dousing like this would leave her magicless until her wings dried out and the dust regenerated.

She didn't realize she'd been holding her breath until the magical river spat her out through some sort of tunnel opening; she only realized it because she could feel cool air on her face instead of water.

"There she is!" she heard Natalie cry.

"Grab her!" Hubble yelled at the same time.

Someone in the darkness caught her around the waist before she smashed onto what seemed to be a rocky, uneven floor. Someone else fumbled for her arm, caught her hand, and wrapped a cloak around her shoulders.

Hubble. He always seemed to be giving her a cloak.

Bellamy shivered. She was cold, but nothing like the soul-chilling freeze she'd experienced in the wake of Tinker's disappearance. "Is everyone all right?" she asked.

"All present and accounted for," said Hubble.

"And all soaked to the bone," said Sam, with much less enthusiasm. Professor Blake's magic control over the boy did not seem to extend past the mirror's event horizon. Bellamy would have been surprised if it had...but not very surprised. "If someone tripped and opened a secret door, it wasn't me."

Bellamy had no idea what Sam was talking about.

"We will only blame you if we're suddenly attacked by a band of teenage girl zombie orcs," Natalie said to her brother. From the tone of her voice, Bellamy could tell Natalie was teasing. "Ugh. Everything is soaked."

"The cloaks stayed dry," Hubble boasted.

"We should have put the matches in with the cloaks," said Sam. "I can't see a thing. What are we supposed to do now?"

"Yeah, Dungeon Master," Natalie said with a great deal of snark. "Whatcha gonna roll to get us out of this one?"

"A natural twenty," Hubble said, followed by what sounded like a deep breath. "Gird your loins, gamers."

Not two seconds later, Hubble *glowed*. His silver skin and hair became as radiant as the moon. The cavern around them began to illuminate as if someone had lit a lantern.

"Whoa," breathed Sam.

"I take it a 'natural twenty' is a good thing," said Bellamy.

"Yes," Natalie confirmed. "It is a very, very good thing. Hubble could you always…glow in the dark?"

Hubble opened his eyes and they gasped—his irises twinkled like sapphires. "All the mine-dwelling kobolds can," he said. "We don't really need it for survival in the modern age, but it does come in handy from time to time."

"I'll say," Sam said with a smile.

"It also burns an incredible amount of energy," Hubble added. "So hand me a snack, willya? And keep 'em coming." Reverently, Sam pulled a granola bar out of his pack and handed it to Hubble. "Thanks. Now," he said as he crunched, "let's hurry up and find a way out of here."

Bellamy surveyed the room. "It seems the only way out is up," she said. "But I won't be able to fly anyone out of here anytime soon."

Hubble tilted his head back and looked up at the gaping hole from which they'd entered. "It's not *that* far up. We might be able to scale it," he said.

"And go where," said Natalie. "Back through the magic mirror?"

"Hey!" Sam, who had been running his hands along the walls, waved them over. "The cavern bends around this way. Come on!"

Excited, they all raced after Sam…but they didn't go far. The tunnel curved into another room, with another gaping hole in the wall about twenty feet up. There, on a rock below the hole, sat a dark-haired boy.

"Well, hello there," he said. "I'm Quin. Welcome to the oubliette."

10

Maker Deng, the Goblin King, sat upon the stone dais. Much like the Mantle of Majesty, his throne was a conglomeration of precious and worthless metals, haphazardly welded together into a structure as strange and imposing as Maker himself. The assembled goblins placed various offerings to the Goblin King around the edge of the dais. Most of the offerings were metal: a slinky, a broken watch, some bolts and washers, a handful of paperclips. Those less fortunate goblins brought the odd fruit or vegetable. Their petitions to the king would be heard last.

Tinker stood at Maker's right hand, learning the art of being a ruler and trying not to hate every moment of it.

Retcher might have been astonished at Tinker's acceptance of his new position, but Maker had exhibited no such surprise. In Maker's eyes, no goblin in his right mind would turn down the magnificent opportunity to be King of the Land and Keeper of Stuff.

Tinker's tenure at Harmswood had taught him that a goblin's "right mind" and everyone else's "right mind" were two very different things.

Maker, as king, was the handsomest of all goblins. He matched Tinker in height, but with none of Tinker's lingering awkwardness. His eyes and hair and flawless skin were all as black as the Myrkwood Mire; that telltale goblin-green hue was almost impossible to make out. Despite his eccentricities, the goblins looked up to Maker as the wisest of the brothers.

Maker had held the position of king far longer than most. Goblin Kings typically retired before the age of thirty. None of them returned to the city after leaving the throne.

Tinker had never really stopped to think about his own mortality before. Allergic or not, who had he been kidding thinking he had a future with Bellamy? Fey lived practically forever. In Goblin City, fifty was old. Sixty was ancient.

Retcher was ancient.

Maker was at least thirty-five, not a Lost "Boy" anymore. He still looked fit as a fiddle, but it was obvious that he was tired. His heart just wasn't in it anymore. He would wax dreamily about far-off lands and white sand beaches...and then play tricks on his brothers or dole out ridiculous punishments purely for his own pleasure.

As yet another assembly began, Tinker wondered absent-mindedly if today would turn out to be a wistfully wise-and-dreamy day, or a wrath-of-an-insane-king day.

"I normally start with a report from the squads," Maker announced without preamble. "But today, some idiot has decided to bring a *cow* into my receiving hall. Pickafur, have you lost what little mind you had to begin with?"

So, not a wistfully wise day then, thought Tinker.

The ragtag bunch of goblins in the hall parted to let Pick-afur and his four-footed friend come forward. The dairy cow's shiny hide was a light brown, and she had kind eyes. Her hooves clacked against the stone floor and the bell around her neck gave a dull clank as she and her master settled in front of the dais.

"Oh, Great and Powerful Goblin King!" Pickafur pulled the hat off his head and held it to his heart. A thick mass of wiry black hair sprang in all directions, as if it, too, had been commanded to stand at attention.

Somehow, Tinker managed to resist smiling.

"Yes?" Maker answered, enjoying the pompous address. "Can I help you, Pickafur?"

"I would very much appreciate it if Your Mightygrand Excellence could please stop that sniveling punk from stealing Esmerelda's candy."

Maker narrowed his eyes and pursed his lips, clearly giving Pickafur's request some thought. Tinker imagined he was making a similar face himself—he had no idea what issue in that sentence to tackle first.

"Esmerelda is...?" Maker asked.

"Our cow, Your Fabulousness." Pickafur gave a quick bow. "The one you had stolen and put in my charge, so that there would always be cream in your coffee and butter on your apple cakes."

"A fine decision, if I do say so myself," said Maker.

"Just so, Your Holiness."

"And exactly which 'sniveling punk' are you referring to? There are a lot of us here. I'm afraid you need to be more specific."

Pickafur raised a baleful finger. One by one, goblins jumped out of the line of his accusatory finger, until one small goblin was left.

"Snot? Here, boy." Maker's command was only a tad less condescending than someone calling for a dog.

Snot wiped his nose on his sleeve and moved forward to stand on the other side of Esmerelda.

"Did you eat Esmerelda's candy?" Maker asked pointedly.

"Yes, Yer Holiface." Snot's attempt at honorifics fell considerably short of Pickafur's. "But I didn't steal nuffin, honest. Essie don't mind sharing 'er candy."

Tinker disguised his laugh as a strange sort of snort.

Maker gave Tinker a sideways glance, but otherwise ignored the outburst. "Pickafur, remind me why we're feeding candy to the cow?"

"Her feed ain't all candy," Pickafur explained. "Just a few treats for dessert after every meal. 'Round All Hallows' Eve, some of the boys got it in their heads that feeding Essie candy bits would turn her milk rainbow colors. Well, it didn't, but Aberdeen did say that the milk was sweeter. So I adjusted her diet, since we don't second-guess Aberdeen when it comes to kitchen business."

"No we do not," Maker agreed.

"So you'll punish the brat, then? Toss him in an oubliette? Dangle him off the parapet? Feed him to the trolls? Give him a right swift kick in the pants?" Pickafur shrugged. "I ain't picky."

Maker leaned back in his throne. "Such a wide range of delights to choose from! But if you don't mind, I think I'll pass this decision down to our king-in-training."

"As you wish, Your Most Splendiforist." Pickafur bowed.

Quick to follow suit, Snot curtsied.

"What do you say, heir apparent?" Maker asked.

Tinker considered the situation. They all expected him to dole out some sort of punishment, that was for sure, but someone else's suffering had never brought Tinker any pleasure. A side effect of Bellamy's influence, to be sure.

Think, you fool. Think. He needed to come up with a punishment that wasn't really a punishment, and quickly.

And then he saw Snot sneak Essie a reassuring pat.

Tinker's heart immediately went out to Snot, a lonely little goblin whose one joy was sharing candy with his best friend the cow. Tinker could almost hear Bellamy in his head: *That poor sweet boy doesn't need a kick in the pants; he needs a hug.*

"Nasty Word!" Tinker called out before his emotions could get the better of him.

"Aye." Nasty Word stepped out of the crowd. He was a rough specimen of goblinhood, with a long, angular face and one eye considerably larger than the other. He was also one of the best goblin squad leaders, second only to Retcher.

"It's not time for the report," Pickafur argued. "You haven't finished with me yet."

"I didn't say I had," Tinker said in as regal a tone as he could muster. "Nasty Word, could you make some room in your unit for Snot?"

"Maybe," Nasty Word said noncommittally.

"Wonderful," said Tinker, because no one refused the Goblin King. Or the almost-Goblin King.

Snot stood tall—being appointed to a goblin squad was a promotion, not a punishment.

Yet.

"In addition to his regular duties," Tinker added, "I'd like to put Snot in charge of candy acquisition. Make sure he collects enough to share with all his brothers."

Snot held his smiling chin so high, Tinker thought the boy might fall over. Pickafur harrumphed. Nasty Word sneered. The rest of the goblins in the room cheered at the prospect of more candy. Tinker caught Maker's eye, and the Goblin King nodded his approval.

For a moment, the cheering reminded Tinker of all the parades Nocturne Falls was famous for. The amount of candy and trinkets thrown into the crowds lining the streets was enough to keep Goblin City in candy for a year. Tinker refrained from mentioning this to the horde, however—all the Falls needed was a sudden influx of wild goblins stealing candy from babies.

Bellamy had performed in every single one of those parades. The year the Harmswood cheering squad had done their routine on a float, Bellamy had spotted Tinker in the crowd and tossed him a salted caramel square—his favorite. She had selected the candy carefully and she hadn't just thrown it to anyone. She'd chosen him.

Oh, Bellamy. His heart ached.

"Well, now that's settled. Pickafur, please get your stinking livestock out of my castle," said the Goblin King. "Nasty Word, what do you have to report?"

As each of the squad leaders reported in, Tinker stepped back to a spot behind Maker's throne. Once he became the true Goblin King, he'd have control of all the magic beneath the city. Somehow, there had to be a way to use that magic to contact Bellamy. Could he conjure something as innocuous as a phone call? How would that work? And even if he found out how to make it work, would she answer? It would be winter break at Harmswood now—had she gone home to her family in South Carolina?

Winter break. Tinker had officially missed all of his midterms. He was actually sad about that. He wondered how the *Romeo and Juliet* skit had gone over at the festival. He wondered if they'd added new seasonal drinks to the Bean's menu. He wondered if the weather had changed.

He wondered if anyone missed him at all.

The melancholy stayed with him until after the audience, when they retired to Maker's chambers. The Goblin King tossed his crown on the table. He ran a hand over his short hair and massaged his temples. "I think that went well. Don't you?"

Tinker shrugged. "I'm trying my best to follow your lead, but I still feel like I'm just making it up as I go along."

Maker gave Tinker a dashing, gap-toothed grin. "I'll tell you a secret: I've been making it all up since the day I got this job."

"Really?" Tinker had a hard time imagining Maker as a young goblin, receiving the Mantle of Majesty and similarly having no idea what to do with it. But he must have been in that situation at some point. The idea that Maker didn't always know exactly what he was going to do next did lift Tinker's spirits.

"Just always remember to have fun." Maker pulled a face at himself in the ornate full-length mirror, and then laughed heartily. "The moment it stops being fun, that's when you know it's time to step down and move on."

Every time Maker mentioned moving on, it sounded like the day was fast approaching. "There's still so much I don't know," said Tinker.

"How long have I been king? There's still a lot *I* don't know," said Maker. "No one warned me that we might recruit a boy who was so smart that his mentor would have to get a scholarship to send him away to school. Though to be fair, Retcher did warn me about you. Maybe that's not the best example. Oh! I know. I had no one around to tell me what to do when intruders came to the city. Had to figure it all out on my own."

"That's because no one in a hundred years or so has ever traveled here to take back a Lost Boy," said Tinker.

"Except now," said Maker.

"*What?!*" Tinker was so surprised he almost screeched the question.

The Goblin King led Tinker back to the table where he'd thrown his crown and pulled away a silk cloth. Beneath it was a crystal ball the size of a large candy apple from Delaney's. Maker picked up the ball and said, "Show me the intruders."

The surface of the crystal went cloudy, silver, and then dark, before lightening to reveal a scene somewhere in the Myrkwood outside the city. Quin Merchero led four figures through the dense trees. One of the bodies was rather short and one was fairly tall. All wore hooded cloaks that shielded their faces from the scrying ball.

Tinker had an inkling who those figures might be, but he was too afraid to hope. "Quin's out of the oubliette?" he asked instead.

"The intruders helped him escape, apparently," said Maker. "As far as I can tell, one's a kobold, one's a wereshifter of some sort, and the other two appear to be human girls. As we don't have any kobolds or weres among the Lost Boys, I can only assume it's the girls who have come to 'rescue' one of our boys."

"Any idea which boy?" Tinker's heart was pounding so hard he could barely breathe. The kobold and the wereshifter—how did Maker know Sam was a were?—could only be Hubble and Sam, which meant the taller of the girls had to be Natalie. Tinker prayed that the other traveler was Bellamy. She didn't have pointed ears, the telltale marker of most fey, so she might have been mistaken for human. There could still be fairy wings hiding under that cloak.

"No idea who they're after," said Maker. "Maybe one of the newer recruits? I could have Nasty or Retcher pull a list together, not that it matters. Besides, I'd think you would be more concerned with Quin coming back to fight you for his rightful place."

"Oh, I am," Tinker lied. "I am absolutely worried about that. What do you suggest I do?"

"Bah. Don't worry," said Maker. "I switched the marker at the last fork they took. Quin thinks he's leading them back to the castle, but I've sent him to the trolls instead. If your luck is good, they'll all be eaten up and you won't have to deal with Quin. Or any of them."

"Joy," Tinker said with no joy at all.

"If your luck is bad, you'll probably end up having to fight Quin to the death." The Goblin King looked almost giddy at the prospect. "I'm incredibly tempted to stick around to see which way it goes! But I've seen goblins fight before. Know what I haven't seen? Butterflies."

In one smooth motion, Maker tossed the crystal ball to Tinker, snapped his fingers, and—with a small bow—stepped backward through the shimmering mirror.

By the time Tinker caught the ball, the Goblin King was gone.

Tinker stared at the crystal ball. Then he stared at the crown on the table. In truth, the Goblin King hadn't gone at all. King Maker Deng had exited Goblin City…and left King Ranulf Tinkerton in his place.

Tinker was now the Goblin King.

He had absolutely no idea what to do.

Ignoring the crown on the table, Tinker sat down in the nearest chair. As of this moment, he was the Goblin King. *I am the Goblin King*, he tried to say aloud, but even thinking it sounded ridiculous. In his hands, the scene still played out inside the crystal ball. The five tiny figures tromped through the Myrkwood, ever closer to their doom.

Bellamy.

The first thing he had to do was stop Bellamy from being eaten by a troll.

"Bellamy!" Tinker screamed at the crystal ball. "Hubble! Sam! Natalie! *Quin!*" Try as he might, no one heard him, not even his goblin brother. Tinker wracked his brain, trying to think of a way to help them. He growled in frustration. Now that he was king, he should be able to harness the magic beneath the city. But how?

Physics.

Magic was a chaotic force, but it still had to follow certain laws of the universe. Laws that he'd studied in school...

There was at least enough magic running through his body to keep the crystal ball activated. He decided he probably shouldn't let it go, in case it stopped working and he couldn't turn it back on again. One by one, he focused on every single one of his friends, trying to communicate. He concentrated on the Myrkwood itself, trying to alter the direction of the path, as Maker had done. He closed his eyes and imagined the magic below the city coming up through the soles of his feet, into his body, out through his hands, and into the crystal sphere.

"Bellamy!"

Nothing.

Tinker paced the room, focused on the crystal. He tried standing and sitting and lying down. He called out every magic spell word from every book he could remember; he even made up some of his own. All he got for his efforts was a splitting headache.

Eventually he laid down with the ball on the pillow beside him. His friends were building a campfire and getting ready to sleep. Quin stood at the edge of the clearing, glancing into the wood with concern.

He knows it's not the right path back to the castle, Tinker thought. *How do I convince him to trust his instincts?*

Tinker wasn't looking forward to a fight with Quin. But he'd rather face a deathmatch than watch the people he loved become a troll's dinner.

His head on the pillow, Tinker began to think about the ball itself. His mind wandered back to Professor Hagar's class, the day after he'd been given the Mantle. The lesson on reflection and refraction. If Tinker could summon even the tiniest bit of magic through the crystal, it was possible that the curve of the sphere would amplify it. If the magic stayed trapped inside the crystal, it might bounce around and amplify further. Totally just a theory, of course. Tinker still couldn't summon any magic at all. But Professor Hagar would have been proud of him for remembering how it was supposed to work.

Exhausted by his efforts, Tinker fell asleep pondering that lesson. Instead of magic, Tinker dreamed that he sent *himself* inside the crystal. He stood over Bellamy's sleeping form. Her cloak was pulled tightly around her body. Shadows of the firelight danced across her face. Tinker bent down to touch her, but his hand passed right through her hair.

Stupid dreams.

"My, my, my."

Tinker whipped his head around. Bellamy's dream-self stood before him in a white silk dress. Her golden hair and luminous wings gleamed like something that belonged on the top of a Christmas tree. And she still wore that tin heart —Tinker's heart—on a ribbon around her neck.

"I've made a wish to dream about you every night since you left us, but this is the first time it's actually happened. What took you so long?"

Tinker rushed to Bellamy and tried to take her in his arms, but it wasn't the same. He could feel the pressure of her dream essence against his, but it was an odd, tingly feeling. Nothing like an actual hug.

"This is so not fair," Tinker groaned.

"I know." Bellamy's dream fingers caressed the essence of his cheek.

"You…you came." He pointed to the bodies sound asleep around the small campfire. "You *all* came. Why?"

"Because you didn't say goodbye." Bellamy smiled mischievously. "Silly boy. *We love you.* There never a question of whether or not we'd come after you. Goodness, the entire school was fightin' over who was gonna bring you back."

"But I...I'm sorry. What about the school?" Surely he hadn't heard her right.

"I'm pretty sure Natalie has video of the whole thing, if you don't believe me. All of Harmswood wanted to come rescue you—students and faculty. We wouldn't even be here without Professor Blake's help. Ranulf Tinkerton, you are loved so much more than you realize."

Tinker didn't think anyone outside this campfire cared for him that much, never mind the Head Witch or anyone else at Harmswood. Under the current circumstances, however, he wasn't sure how much it mattered any more.

"Bellamy"—it was so annoying not to be able to take her hand!—"I'm king now."

Her hands flew to her face and her wings fluttered. "Oh my goodness! Since when?"

"A few hours ago, maybe? It all happened so fast."

Futile as it was, Bellamy's dream-self hugged him again anyway. "Tinker, that's wonderful! I am so proud of you. We'll be at the castle soon, and you can tell us all about it! I guess this means we can't properly rescue you, and that's a shame. Everyone at school will be so disappointed. But we'll be able to set up some proper lines of communication, won't we? King or not, Mister Tinkerton, I refuse to let you be gone from me forever. There has to be a way for us to keep in touch."

Tinker was so overwhelmed by the sheer Bellamy-ness of her answer that he almost lost control of the dream. They'd been apart for such a short time, but he missed her light and optimism like a choking man missed oxygen.

Tinker also knew Bellamy better than he knew himself. The rapid-fire pace of her congratulations meant she was nervous. Finding out he was already king devastated her as much as it did him, but she'd still put a positive spin on it. She'd also thrown him an easy way out of their relationship with all her talk of "keeping in touch."

"Bellamy," he interrupted. "I don't want to be king."

"You don't?"

"No. I never did. I want to go back to school. I want to be with you." He put his dream hand on hers and merged their essence. "I want to be rescued."

The smile she gave him then mended every crack in his broken heart.

"I don't know enough about the goblin magic yet to be able to bring you straight to the city. I'm sorry."

"That's all right." The tone of her voice was so very sweet. "We've made it this far; we can make it the rest of the way."

Not if they got eaten by trolls first. "Bellamy, the Goblin King changed the direction of your path before he left. You're going the wrong way. Quin knows it."

"Quin. He was the one who was supposed to be king, wasn't he? I guessed that."

"Yes," said Tinker. "So…any chance he still wants the job?"

Bellamy nodded. "Oh, yes. I think so."

For the first time in a long time, Tinker felt the first stirrings of relief. "I suspect he still has more of an affinity with the goblin magic than I do. Just please tell him to trust his instincts."

"I will."

"But before you come to the castle at all, I need to ask you a really important question." Now that he had her alone, away from Hubble and school and everyone else, there was no better time to have this conversation.

"Of course! Ask away."

"I've had some time to think while I've been here and I realized: you and I have always been pawns in someone else's game. We were thrown together when we were just kids, and we keep being thrown together. Hubble orchestrated that whole thing at the masquerade—"

"My sister had a hand in that too," Bellamy mumbled.

"—even Professor Blake got you here. But there are reasons goblins and fairies aren't supposed to be together, beyond the allergy thing. I mean, you're going to live a long and fruitful life; I'll be lucky to get another fifty good years."

Bellamy's brow furrowed. It was obvious she hadn't stopped to do that math either.

"The day we met, you looked at me and didn't see a pathetic, sniveling goblin boy, you saw the amazing person I could be. You saw the Goblin King before I even became him. Loving you meant never being able to hug you or hold your hand or wipe away your tears or kiss you beneath a starry sky, but for me, just being with you was enough. If we could only meet like this, in our dreams, forever, I would sleep my life away."

There were dream-tears in Bellamy's eyes. "Tinker, what are you askin' me?"

"Do you *want* to be with me? We became friends because we were victims of circumstance—maybe we still are. And I might have an idea about how to make things work out. But I don't want to do anything until I know that you've come all the way to Goblin City because you *want* to be with me, not just because you *can*."

"Oh, Tinker." Bellamy shook her head; the dream curls of her rainbow-streaked hair floated around her in slow motion. "All I know is, I love you. Maybe everyone else had somethin' to do with us meetin' and maybe not. But I have loved you since that moment, and lovin' you was no one's decision but mine."

Tinker smiled at the fairy who loved him. "I really want to kiss you right now."

"So do I," she said. "Soon. In the meantime, tell me a little bit about your plan. Are you goin' to give the crown back to Quin?"

"Seems like a better plan than fighting to the death," he said. "But the goblins as a people still need a lot of help. Having lived most of my life outside Goblin City, I can see the issues so clearly now. I think I can serve the goblins best if I become a bridge between the Goblin King and the outside world. I'm just… I'm just not sure about the details."

"I suspect Professor Blake would be happy to help you," said Bellamy.

"I hadn't thought about that, but considering what you've told me, I think talking to her is a good first step."

"So what will you be instead of king?" Bellamy asked. "You'll need a new title. Somethin' important."

"Negotiator, maybe? Mediator? Ambassador? I don't know."

"I have a suggestion." Bellamy smirked. "How about 'Boyfriend?'"

Tinker laughed. After all they'd been through, the boyfriend/girlfriend thing was the one question he still hadn't managed to ask her. He pretended to mull it over. "Hmm. 'Ambassador-Boyfriend' does have a certain ring to it."

Bellamy scowled playfully. "Maybe I won't be kissin' you when we get to the castle after all."

Tinker mimed being stabbed in the chest, flailing about until Bellamy giggled.

"Seriously, though," Tinker said soberly. "It's very important that you remember to turn everyone back as soon as you wake up from this dream. A troll might have caught your scent already, and if one has, I don't know how to stop it."

"A troll?" Bellamy tilted her head and put her hands on her hips. "Oh, honey. You just let me deal with it. I got this."

11

Bellamy woke up feeling like a new person. Or, rather, she felt like her old self again. She remembered every moment of the dream she'd shared with Tinker. As she moved through her morning stretches, she recalled the touching conversation they'd had and the exciting decisions they'd made. The memory alone was enough to dust off the cobwebs that had been settling since Tinker had received his marching orders, and now the sun was shining in her soul again.

Bellamy Merriweather Larousse was back, and in fighting form. These goblins wouldn't know what hit them!

First, of course, Bellamy would have to deal with Hubble. And Quin. And maybe trolls. She couldn't decide which one would be the most fun.

Bellamy sorted through the bag of snacks while the rest of her fellow travelers slept. As far as she could tell, Quin still didn't know she was a fairy. She'd kept her cloak on, even when making that painstaking climb up the side of the oubliette. Had they waited until her wings dried out, she could have simply flown herself and everyone else out of the cavernous prison…but she didn't want to wait. So she'd put her cheerleading muscles to work and pulled her water-logged self up that wall to the tunnel that led to the Myrk-wood, just like everyone else.

Bellamy also suspected Quin had no idea that his fellow travelers knew he was the former heir to the goblin throne. He'd introduced himself as "Keen" instead of "Quinn"—Bellamy had only ever seen his name written down in Tinker's note, so it was a while before she realized she'd assumed the wrong pronunciation. He wasn't allergic to Bellamy, and his hair and eyes were dark and his skin had naturally brown tones. The setting sun, however, turned all his features a particular shade of green. And he seemed, despite a naturally pessimistic nature, to be incredibly proud about showing them the way to Goblin City.

Once Bellamy had put it all together, she'd pulled Hubble aside and let him in on the secret.

"I knew all this 'leading us to Goblin City as thanks for helping him escape' was too good to be true," Hubble said. "He's planning to betray us to the Goblin King in an effort to get his place back from Tinker."

Bellamy nodded. "That's what I thought, too. It makes the most sense."

"Well, let him keep thinking he's pulled the wool over our eyes," said Hubble. "And stay vigilant about hiding your wings. If he knows he's delivering a dreaded fey to the doorstep of his king, he might change his mind."

Bellamy considered their exchange as she walked down to the stream to refill the canteens. Hubble had imparted Quin's secret to Natalie and Sam, as well as the expectation of his betrayal. They had both taken it in stride. Well...once Natalie had been convinced that it wouldn't be in their best interests to kill Quin in his sleep, she had taken it in stride.

It was nice to have the upper hand for once.

Bellamy brought the water to a boil in the saucepan.

From her magic pocket she pulled a small bag of coffee grounds she'd secretly brought along from the Bean. She had figured they'd need coffee at some point, and it was nice to be reminded of home.

One by one, the rest of the travelers awoke as the aroma of pumpkin spice filled the air. One by one, Bellamy poured them each a paper cup of hot coffee. Except Sam. He rolled into a sitting position around the fire, eyes closed, hair sticking straight up on one side.

"Darlin', you look like you've been hit by a Mack truck," Bellamy said to him.

"I feel like it," he mumbled.

"Hair of the dog?" Bellamy offered.

Natalie shook her head vigorously over her own cup of coffee.

Sam leaned forward and inhaled the lovely steam rising out of the saucepan. Then he groaned. "I'll stick with water, thanks."

Hubble shoved a canteen into Sam's hand and he drank deeply. "I'm surprised you didn't go full were after that major buzz you had yesterday," Hubble said to him.

"So am I," said Natalie. "You're gaining more control, bro. Proud of you."

"Thanks, sis," Sam muttered.

"Muffin?" Bellamy offered to Quin.

The ex-goblin prince scrutinized the cellophane package, but took a muffin anyway. "Do you guys do this sort of thing every morning?"

"What thing?" Hubble asked obtusely.

"This whole…breakfast thing."

"We do when Bellamy's around," said Natalie.

"We love Bellamy," Sam said sleepily.

"Aw, thank you, sweetie," Bellamy said to Sam. "We call it 'southern hospitality,'" she said to Quin.

"Whatever you call it, we should drink up and get moving," said Quin. "We've got a long road ahead."

"Yes we do." Bellamy leaned back against a log and sipped her coffee with exceeding slowness. "Just not that road."

Quin, in the middle of a swallow, almost did a spit take. "Excuse me?"

Bellamy raised a hand. "Now, I'm not one to go tellin' anybody their business," she said. "You are absolutely welcome to go that way, if you wish. Just don't look back and expect to see me behind you."

"What is going on?" Sam whispered to Natalie.

"I have no idea," whispered Natalie, "but I love it."

"There are games afoot," Hubble said under his breath.

Quin stood up, spilling his coffee. "Look, you said you wanted to get to the Goblin City. That"—he pointed down the dark path through the trees—"is the way to Goblin City. You can follow me or not, I don't care."

Bellamy nibbled daintily on a muffin. "Have it your way," she said. "But I imagine it'll be difficult takin' the goblin throne back from Tinker once your head's been ripped off by a troll."

Quin, sputtering, sat back down. "You...you know about me?"

Bellamy sipped her coffee. "I know a lot of things."

"She's a witch," said Sam.

"She's a goddess," said Hubble.

"She's a southern belle," said Natalie.

"For instance," said Bellamy, "I know that Tinker is now the Goblin King."

"What?" Hubble cried.

Bellamy's voice became solemn. "Which means that challengin' him now will result in a fight to the death."

"That is the way of our people," said Quin.

"But it's not Tinker's way," said Bellamy. "You'd know that

if you knew him like we do. He doesn't want that. In fact, he doesn't want the crown at all."

Quin clenched his jaw. "Now I know you're lying. No goblin gives up the throne, ever."

"Tinker would," said Natalie.

"Yup," Sam agreed with a yawn.

"But why?" Quin asked. "What on earth could possibly be better than being King of all Goblins? Certainly not *school.*" He said the word as if it smelled like bad cheese.

"True love," Hubble answered. "The most powerful force in the universe."

He and Bellamy exchanged smiles.

"That's ridiculous," said Quin. "Even if what you say is true, Tinker's going to what, just hand over the crown, just like that?"

Bellamy shrugged. "Not if you die first." She finished off her muffin. "*That* way leads to Goblin City. *That* way leads to trolls. And you know it."

Quin stood again. He walked ahead to the path he'd been meaning to follow, and then back toward the way they'd come. He touched the trees, sniffed the air.

"You might be—" Quin might have finished the sentence if a troll hadn't materialized out of the dense brush and grabbed him from behind.

"CRUNCH HAVE YOU NOW!" The troll roared in triumph.

Natalie, Sam and Hubble immediately sprang into action. Hubble grabbed one of the troll's arms and tried to pull it away from Quin. Natalie came up from behind, yanking the troll's flaming red hair and wrapping her arms around his neck in an effort to choke him. Sam took the low ground, lying on the ground and rolling his own body toward them in an effort to take out the troll's legs. As one, the whole mess of them came tumbling to the ground.

Bellamy stood, folded her arms across her chest and waited. Sipped her coffee. Tapped her foot.

Eventually, the screams and roars and pulling and punching stopped. They all stared at Bellamy staring at them. Quin and the others stepped away from the troll.

The troll bared his teeth and growled at Bellamy.

Bellamy didn't even flinch. "Really, Mr. Troll. I am disappointed."

"AM NOT MISTER TROLL," bellowed the troll. "AM CRUNCH THE BASHER, SON OF SMASHER AND CRASHER AND TERROR OF MYRKWOOD!"

Crunch the Basher's breath smelled worse than the bog. It made Bellamy's eyes tear up, but she managed to maintain her poised look of disdain. "Basher… Any relation to Dimshall Basher?"

"Him my uncle," Crunch said at a more tolerable volume. "Him sent away to far-off land. Never see again."

"Then you know Ugh and D'ugh, of course." Now that Bellamy had a good look at Crunch, she realized he was quite a young troll, similar in age to the troll twins who lived down the street. He even had the same bulbous nose.

"Ugh and D'ugh am cousins! How you know Ugh and D'ugh?"

"That far-off land your uncle was sent to? My family lives there."

"You pulling Crunch's leg!"

"I assure you, Mr. Basher, I wouldn't even if I could. Care for a snack?" Bellamy held out a package of powdered donuts.

"She's giving him our snacks?" Sam asked incredulously.

"Bellamy…" Hubble warned.

Bellamy held her hand out flat beside her—not enough to be threatening to the troll, but enough for her friends to know that she meant for them to stay out of this.

The troll began to reach for the package, and then thought better of it. He growled at Bellamy again. "Crunch no snack on human food. CRUNCH SNACK ON FACE."

Daintily, Bellamy wiped the spittle off her cheek. "Trolls don't eat people anymore."

"YOU LYING TO CRUNCH."

"Oh, dear." Bellamy clicked her tongue. "I suspect your village or town or what-have-you probably just hasn't gotten the memo way out here in the Myrkwood, but none of the trolls I know eat people anymore. I don't think they have for quite some time. Generations, even."

"What trolls eat if no people?" Crunch asked.

"Vegetables, mostly," said Bellamy. "Cucumbers, tomatoes… Squash, especially. Zucchini, butternut, yellow, pumpkins…pretty much all the gourds."

"What *gourd*?" The word became at least three syllables as Crunch tried to wrap his giant tongue around it. The attempt was almost charming.

"The gourd is a fascinatin' plant that comes in a variety of shapes and colors," said Bellamy. "A lot like people. When I get back home, I'll be sure to send you some."

"You send present to Crunch from far-off land?"

"Of course I will!" Bellamy said. "Sending presents is something friends do. You are my friend, aren't you?"

Crunch squinted one eye to look at Bellamy, and then the other. "You friend of Ugh and D'ugh?"

"I am," she said confidently. "My name is Bellamy." She offered the package of donuts again.

This time he took it. "Hello, friend Bellamy. I Crunch. Nice meet you."

"It is lovely to meet you too, Crunch. We were just havin' breakfast. Won't you join us by the fire?"

Bellamy waited for Crunch to settle himself before taking a place at his side. Slowly, the rest of them sat down as well, a little worse for wear. Quin's hair and clothes were completely rumpled, and he winced as he straightened them. Hubble had a bite mark on his arm; Natalie had a long scratch down one cheek. And Bellamy wasn't sure, but it looked like Sam was developing a black eye.

"I don't believe I'm doing this right now," muttered Quin.

"Me neither," said Sam. "This is nowhere in the D&D handbook."

"Anything is possible in Bellamy's world," said Natalie. "We're playing by her handbook now."

Hubble drained the rest of his cup of coffee in one gulp and said nothing.

"If you wouldn't mind, Crunch, we could use your help," Bellamy said.

"How Crunch help new friend?"

"We're a little lost. See, we're tryin' to get to Goblin City, but I think we're goin' the wrong way." She pointed down the dark path through the trees. It looked a little less scary now.

Crunch put a large hand on his substantial belly and laughed. "That no way to Goblin City! That way to troll village or town or what-have-me."

"So we should go back the way we came?" Bellamy pointed in the opposite direction.

Crunch laughed again. "That way a very long way. Use shortcut to Goblin City. Take boat."

"There's a boat?" Hubble and Quin asked at the same time.

"Come. Crunch show you." The troll stood up and proceeded to stomp through the trees and brush, making a path where there had been none before. Quickly, Bellamy and her companions gathered up their things and kicked sand over the fire. Single file, they followed along behind Crunch.

"He's leading us to our doom," said Quin.

"If that's the case, I'd really like to take a nap first," said Sam. "But I don't think he is."

"Bellamy has a tendency to bring out the best in people," Natalie told Quin.

As promised, Crunch's path did empty out onto a small strip of beach, where an empty canoe had been beached. There were a couple of paddles on the shore, a few shoes, and what looked like the remnants of several bags of supplies. Sam and Natalie quickly began to sift though the wreckage, gathering up anything they might need.

Hubble examined the canoe. "It looks sound. I think it will float."

Bellamy shook her head over the scene. "Do I even need to ask what happened here?"

The troll hung his head. "Crunch make sure village or what-have-me gets memo about not eating people."

"Thank you, Crunch," said Bellamy. "I do appreciate you passin' that along."

"Crunch sad now," said the troll. "He too big to go in boat with new friend Bellamy."

Bellamy cupped the large troll's cheek in her tiny hand. "I promise to send a case of squashes to your village. Maybe even two."

"Bellamy say hello to Ugh and D'ugh for Crunch?"

"I absolutely will," she said as she got into the boat. "Thank you so much, Crunch. I will never forget this."

"Neither will I," said Quin.

"Or me," said Sam.

"We will tell the story of Crunch the Basher from sea to shining sea," Hubble said grandly.

"Crunch like that," said the troll. "Goodbye, friends." And with a great push, he sent the canoe off into the lake.

All the companions waved a hearty goodbye to the troll.

"I'm not sure anyone would believe me if I told them what just happened," said Quin.

Bellamy turned to the former prince. "Do you know where we are now?" she asked impatiently.

"I think so," he said. "I had no idea we were this close to the water's edge, or I would have led us here myself."

"But you couldn't have known about the canoe," said Natalie.

"Good point," said Quin.

Bellamy continued to scan the edges of the water, but there was no clue as to where their destination might be.

"Goblin City should be just around that bend," Quin said.

Bellamy's eyes met Hubble's. She didn't need his permission for what she was about to do, but she'd feel better with his blessing. Hubble didn't even have to ask. He smiled at her and shook his head. "I hope that one day I find a girl who loves me half as much as you love that goblin brat of ours," he said. "Go on. We'll be right behind you."

Careful to maintain her balance—much like being atop a cheer pyramid—Bellamy stood up in the canoe. She let her cloak fall away and spread her wings, now fully-dry and reenergized. With one great leap she lifted herself into the air, leaving a trail of colorful dust in her wake so large that she wouldn't have been surprised to see the canoe and everyone in it floating behind her.

As soon as she had risen above the treeline, she saw the top of the castle, the keep walls, and the sprawling city beyond it. She headed straight for the topmost tower. There was a room there with a large bed and an ornate mirror; Bellamy flew in through an open window and took a look around. She spotted the Mantle of Majesty and the goblin mask Tinker had worn to the ball, but there was no sign of Tinker himself.

She leapt out the window and caught another air current

beneath her wings. She followed the sounds of animals to a cow shed and a henhouse, but still no Tinker. She flew down an alleyway, stopping only when she came across an open doorway, through which emerged the most wonderful smell.

"Tinker?" Bellamy called into the room.

"King Ranulf is not here at the moment," replied a voice from within. "Can I help you, miss?" Gingerly, an aproned goblin felt his way into the doorway, but he did not venture out into the street.

Bellamy kept her distance. "You must be Aberdeen, the brilliant chef! Tinker's told me so much about you."

"I'm afraid you have me at a disadvantage," the chef replied politely. He held out a hand. "Come here, child, so I can see you better."

"I can't," she said quickly. "My name is Bellamy, and I'm fey. I don't want to hurt you."

"Have you come here to hurt our king?" Aberdeen asked.

"I've come here because I love him," Bellamy said with all her heart. "Please, can you tell me where I might find him?"

"He is in the receiving hall," said Aberdeen. "All the way down to the end of this street and then right a ways. It is a large building with windows that face west."

Bellamy had thought Aberdeen was blind. "How would you know that?"

"Because the place echoes like a cave and grows incredibly warm in the afternoon."

"You are truly as amazin' as Tinker says, Chef Aberdeen. Thank you."

"I suspect you are quite amazing yourself, fey child," said the chef.

When Bellamy was a safe distance from the kitchen, she launched herself into the air again and flew down the street. The building that matched Aberdeen's description had a large door manned by two goblin guards in colorful armor. They crossed their spears before her as she approached.

"No one sees the king without an appointment," said one of the guards.

"Especially no one with wings," said the other.

"My sincerest apologies, gentlemen," Bellamy said. Then she shook her wings enough to send both of the guards into sneezing fits. Once they had fallen away, she pushed open the doors so hard that they slammed against the walls. The assembly of goblins turned as one.

Tinker, standing before the throne at the other end of the hall, smiled. It was the most beautiful sight she had ever seen.

"Ranulf Tinkerton, Goblin King!" Bellamy cried. "I seek an audience with you!"

Tinker put his hands on his hips. "You sure do know how to make a grand entrance."

"I learned from the best."

"Hubble?" he guessed.

"As I live and breathe," said Bellamy.

"So what happens now?"

Bellamy spread her wings. "Brace yourself."

Some of the goblins in the room ran away. Some of them ducked. Some of them simply stared, stunned as Bellamy soared over their heads and crashed right into their king.

Tinker's body was warm and solid and smelled like apples. As they wrapped their arms around each other, she felt him laugh into her hair.

"Definitely not a dream," he said.

"No," she laughed with him. "This is definitely not a dream." She pulled back, staring into that face she had missed so much. He was ten times handsomer than when she'd last seen him, if that were even possible.

"Permission to kiss the king?" she asked.

"Permission granted," he said, meeting her lips halfway.

"Ewwwwwwwwwww," Bellamy heard Tinker's goblin brothers jeer, amid a chorus of sneezes.

They kissed over and over, never wanting to stop. The ball of sunshine inside her burned even brighter. No matter how they had come together, no matter whose fingers had stirred the pot, and no matter what happened from this moment on, Bellamy and Tinker had chosen each other.

This was how it was supposed to be.

12

With Bellamy back in his arms, everything was right in Tinker's world. There would be no Goblin King stopping him this time—he was the Goblin King now. If it were up to him, he'd never let this beautiful, amazing, adventurous and crazy fairy go again. Ever.

"Attention, everyone!" Tinker heard a voice—Hubble?—announce to the gathering of goblins. "Your king will be right back with you after a short recess. Thank you for your patience!" Hubble poked Tinker in the side. He must have poked Bellamy too, because she winced and scowled at the kobold. "Come on, lovebirds," Hubble whispered. "Let's go."

"Go where?" Tinker asked.

"I don't know," said Hubble. "This is a stage, isn't it? That means it has some sort of backstage. Wherever that is, go there."

There was a door, off to one side of the dais, that led to a small chamber. The chamber, in turn, led to a series of secret tunnels that the king could use to get anywhere in the castle. Hubble prodded Tinker and Bellamy into the chamber. Three hooded figures slipped in after him.

As their hoods fell back, Tinker realized that it wasn't just Bellamy who wore a piece of tin from the Mantle of Majesty. Tinker's eyes misted at the sentiment. His very own Harmswood squad. Those necklaces, and the people who wore them, were the most priceless treasures in the goblin kingdom, bar none.

"Sam! Natalie!" Tinker stepped away from Bellamy long enough to hug his friends. "I can't believe you came!"

"Believe it," said Sam. The poor kid had huge dark circles under both eyes. Tinker wondered what horrible circumstances they'd had to endure that he hadn't seen in the crystal ball.

"Between these two, it's not like we had much of a choice." Natalie waggled her thumb between Hubble and Bellamy.

"Come here, you silver-tongued devil." Tinker pulled Hubble to him and tousled his hair. "You successfully got a party of misfits through the dungeon in one piece! I'm so proud."

"Oh, shut up." Hubble gave him a half-hearted shove. "It's not like you wouldn't have done the same thing in my place, *Your Majesty*."

"That's right," said Natalie. "Are we supposed to bow to you or something?"

"Please don't," said Tinker.

"Hey, did you know Hubble could glow in the dark?" Sam interjected.

Tinker raised an eyebrow. "I did know. I'm surprised *you* know. That's not exactly a talent he advertises."

"We could not have escaped the oubliette without him," said Quin.

For the first time, Tinker shifted his focus to the former Goblin Prince. He wasn't sure whether or not to punch

Quin's ruggedly handsome face, or hug him. Since he was in an incomparably good mood, he chose the latter.

"We picked up a stray," said Hubble.

"I'm very glad you did," said Tinker. "Because the goblins are going to need someone to lead them after I go back to Harmswood."

Quin's brow furrowed and he looked to Bellamy.

She flashed him that amazing smile. "I told you he didn't want the crown."

"I honestly don't," said Tinker. "I never did. The throne was always meant to be yours, and I'd be more than happy to give it to you now. If you would accept it."

"I…" Quin seemed at a loss for words. "Yes, I will. Of course I will. It's just…"

For a moment, Tinker forgot how to breathe. Everything was going so well, even better than he planned. He should have known Quin of all people would screw it all up. "What is it, Quin? I'm giving you the crown you've lived your whole life for. What more do you want?"

Quin held his head with the natural regal bearing of a king. If Tinker continued to be king for a hundred years, he wasn't sure he'd ever get that down. "I want to go to school too," he said. "With you." He pointed to the rest of Tinker's friends. "With them."

"Seriously?" asked Natalie.

"I take that as a compliment," said Bellamy.

Sam yawned. "I think that would be kind of cool actually."

Hubble just laughed.

"Wait," said Tinker. "Why would you want to go to a place you've never been? Do you know anything about school at all?"

"I know it's important to you," Quin said seriously. "So important that you'd give up the throne for it. I know that I'd be able to learn things there—greater knowledge can only make me a better king."

Tinker certainly couldn't argue with that logic.

"And Harmswood seems to house some of the most extraordinary people," Quin added. "If the rest of the student body are anything like these three, I'd be stupid not to go. I want the chance to have friends like this." He looked at Bellamy again. "Even if they're fey."

Tinker put his arms around Bellamy and Hubble and squeezed them both. "I can honestly say that there is no one on earth like the people in this room," Tinker boasted. "But I'm inclined to agree with you. I think a few years at Harmswood would do you—and the goblins as a whole—a great deal of good."

"But who will lead the goblins if both of you come back with us?" asked Bellamy.

It was a good question. Tinker forced his brain to think. With no Maker Deng to guide him, who would he have turned to as king if there was an emergency? Who did most of the goblins look up to anyway?

Tinker poked his head back into the receiving hall. "Snot!"

The tiny goblin scurried up to him and saluted. "Yes, Yer Royalnose?"

Well, at least his addresses were improving. "Run up to my chamber and bring down the Mantle of Majesty. It's very important. Can you do that?"

Without a word, the goblin scurried away. Tinker hoped he could take that as a yes. He turned back to the room and hugged Bellamy again. "I have to do this one last thing without you," he said, "and I really don't want to let you go."

"It's all right," she said with that beautiful look of under-standing. "If I go back out there, I'll just be a distraction."

"Not to mention hazardous to everyone's health," said Hubble.

"He's right," said Bellamy. "You go take care of business. I'll be here waiting for you."

Tinker wished he had a recording of those words, so that he could hear her say them over and over. He kissed her quickly, and then once more, because the first time wasn't enough. "We'll leave as soon as I get back."

"Sam and I will stay with her," said Natalie. Sam looked to tired too do anything but nod.

Tinker turned to Quin and Hubble. "Okay, let's do this."

Hubble exited the door first and walked out to the edge of the dais. "Hear ye, hear ye!" he cried, but the roar of chattering goblins did not diminish. "LISTEN UP!" he yelled. That seemed to do it. "Your king has an announcement to make."

Tinker walked out on the dais with Quin right behind him. There were simultaneous gasps and jeers at Quin's appearance.

"Whatze doin' here?"

"Traitor!"

"Pretty Boy!"

Tinker held up a hand. "My goblin brothers," he said into the crowd. "You know I was never meant to be your king."

"But I voted for you!" yelled one goblin.

"Me too!" yelled another.

"I didn't!" yelled a third.

Tinker ignored the outbursts. "I believe that exiling Quin Merchero was an emotional choice made by our former king."

"Long live the king!" cried Nasty Word. Tinker noticed that Snot had returned to the hall. He stood dutifully behind his new squad leader. There was a burlap sack in his hands and an artistic green goblin masquerade mask perched on his forehead.

"I would like to reinstate Quin Merchero as your rightful Goblin King."

A murmur washed over the crowd. "Then what will *you* do?" one brother asked.

"Ready to retire already?" asked another.

"I will return to Harmswood Academy and continue my studies there," said Tinker. "I will also serve under the new king as his ambassador to Goblin City. I will work tirelessly to improve conditions here, so that we can one day live in peace without having to steal everything we need to survive."

The goblins didn't seem quite sure what to do with that statement.

"Candy for everyone!" yelled Snot.

"CANDY FOR EVERYONE!" the goblins cheered.

"But in order to make this new job work, I need Quin to come to Harmswood with me for a while," Tinker said to the goblins. "In light of that, we must name a Goblin King Regent to rule over everyone and make decisions on Quin's behalf during his absence. I'd like to suggest Retcher as my nominee. Retcher, would you come up here please?"

Retcher, shaking his head, stepped away from the rest of the goblin squad leaders and joined Tinker beside the throne. There was cheering and his name was called from every corner of the room. Snot followed Retcher up onto the dais and handed Tinker the burlap sack, and then returned to his spot behind Nasty Word.

Nasty Word looked less than pleased.

"The student surpasses the master," Retcher whispered to Tinker. "You're a clever boy."

"I learned from the best," he whispered back. "We will now put it to a vote," Tinker announced to the crowd. "All in favor of Retcher becoming interim king, raise your hand."

As suspected, almost all the goblins in the room raised their hands.

Tinker pulled the Mantle of Majesty out of the sack. "Retcher of the Goblins," he said, "I hereby bestow upon you the Mantle of Majesty. Henceforth, you will be known as the Goblin King Regent, until the rightful king returns from school."

Tinker settled the clanking Mantle on the head of his mentor. He swore he saw Retcher's bent form straighten ever so slightly. With any luck, this Mantle would also give Retcher the same health it had imbued in Tinker. One less worry for his frazzled heart.

"I promise to rule to the best of my abilities," Retcher said without having to clear his throat. "I will be fair, but firm. I will make both of our Goblin Kings proud. I will make all of Goblin City proud!"

More cheers and cries of "candy for everyone" echoed through the hall.

"See you later, everybody!" Quin said with a wave, and then hopped off the dais.

Hubble bowed deeply to Retcher before doing the same.

"Good luck with everything," Tinker said to Retcher. "Not that you'll need it. But good luck all the same. I'll see you next summer." He bent down to embrace his mentor.

Retcher squeezed him tightly. "Not if I don't summon you back here first." He laughed, and patted Tinker on the cheek. "Love you, son. Proud of you. Now you kids get your butts back to school. And be good to that fairy!"

Joyfully, Tinker squeezed Retcher one more time, and then followed Quin and Hubble off the dais and through the "backstage" door. As promised, Bellamy was waiting for him, and Natalie, and…

"Where's Sam?"

Natalie lifted the cloak on the ground to reveal a sloth, fast asleep. "You get to carry him home," said Natalie.

"With pleasure." Tinker laughed and scooped up his furry friend. He took Bellamy's hand, kissed the back of it, and began bounding up the stairs.

Home, Natalie had said. They were going home. Tinker's other home. And never again would he have to choose between the two.

~

When Tinker returned to the mostly-empty common room, his friends were waiting. *His friends.* If you had asked him to count his friends a few weeks ago, he would have been able to do it on one hand. Now he counted everyone at Harmswood, in varying degrees. Natalie made him watch the video she had taken of the mob scene after the ball. All those voices rallying behind Bellamy, on his behalf, was irrefutable evidence of just how much he belonged in Nocturne Falls.

Tinker's heart was as warm as the blazing hearth before him. The people who waited on the couches there weren't just his friends anymore. They were family.

Bellamy perched on the corner of an ottoman; Tinker popped down in the chair beside her. "My head is killing me," he said. "How long was I in there for this time?"

"Three hours," said Natalie.

"Almost four," said Hubble.

Bellamy scooted over enough so that their legs were touching. Despite the excellent quality of their kisses, she and Tinker had decided against flagrant displays of affection while on school grounds. But they still couldn't stand to be apart from each other if they didn't have to, so they made sure to maintain some sort of physical contact whenever they could. Tinker knew this phase of their relationship was probably a result of everything they'd been through, and it probably wouldn't last...but Bellamy's presence brought him a great deal of comfort, and he needed that right now.

"So what did you and Professor Blake talk about?" Bellamy asked.

"Dean Zuru joined us for this session," said Tinker. "I have a week to make up my midterms. While I'm doing that, Quin will be given aptitude tests to gauge where his strengths lie academically."

"I get to stay?" Quin asked eagerly.

"You get to stay." Tinker nodded his head. It hurt to even do that. "Apparently, Harmswood would be proud to foster more boys as clever and forward thinking as me."

"They really said that?" asked Natalie.

"Wow," said Hubble.

"They're talking about sending some teachers to Goblin City to give a few aptitude tests there. Professor Van Zant offered to put together a team for that. While that was on the table I mentioned the outreach programs I proposed before: first aid, animal husbandry, geology...things the Lost Boys really need to learn on the city grounds. And...there was so much more. I'm glad Professor Blake called a stop for today. I was on the verge of passing out right there on the dean's desk."

"You could always join Sam," said Natalie. "He's still sleeping off our adventure. Stinky were-butt."

"I envy him," said Tinker.

Bellamy took his hand. "Can we get you some coffee? Tea?"

Tinker winced. "No tea," he said. "I've had enough of Dean Zuru's tea to float all the way back to Goblin City."

Bellamy stood behind his chair and began to massage his temples. It felt divine. "I know you're exhausted, but it sounds like you're doin' really well at this whole Ambassador thing," she said softly. "Retcher would be so proud."

Eyes closed in bliss, Tinker smiled. "Ambassador-*Boyfriend*," he clarified. "I'm sure Retcher would be proud of that too."

"Of course he would," said Hubble. "Especially after all the trouble he went to setting the two of you up in the first place."

Tinker's eyes flew open. Bellamy's fingers stopped making their gentle circles on his head.

"Why are you both looking at me like that?" Hubble asked. "You're weirding me out."

"Retcher raised me and facilitated my admission to Harmswood," said Tinker. "He'd never been here before. There was no way he could have known I'd become best friends with Bellamy. I didn't even tell him about my feelings for her until last summer."

"Shortly after which, you found yourself tapped to become Goblin King, the one man in all of Goblin City who can touch a fairy without being poisoned. Convenient, don't you think?"

Bellamy slid down to sit on the arm of Tinker's chair, hand over her mouth.

Natalie twisted the bit of tin on her necklace as she eyed them both. "You never put that together? Neither of you?"

Tinker shook his head. Beside him, Bellamy did the same.

"I may be a great director," said Hubble, "but I could take a few pointers from that guardian of yours. He's the tops."

That explained Hubble's deep bow to Retcher before leaving the Goblin City! Tinker had been wondering what prompted that, but he'd ultimately written it off as a general show of respect on behalf of the flamboyant kobold.

"I don't know," Natalie said. "I'd say dressing them both in costume and shoving them in a snow globe ranks pretty high up there as well."

"Thank you," Hubble mimed tipping the brim of an invisible hat.

"I still haven't heard that whole story," said Quin. "Looking forward to it."

Bellamy's hand dropped into Tinker's chair and he slid his fingers in between hers. His dark green eyes met her brilliant blue ones, and he knew what was going through her mind without even speaking. They'd had this conversation once before, in a dream, where they discussed being pawns in everyone else's games. They had chosen to be together. Bellamy, sitting here beside him now and holding his hand, was still choosing to be with him.

"Hey, Tinkerton!"

Tinker looked up to see a small pack of wolf-shifters passing through the common room. He mustered up the energy to respond with a decent amount of enthusiasm. "Hey! What are you guys doing back so soon?"

"Snow," they said in unison.

"My family decided to go to Aspen," said one were.

"Mine are in Stowe," said another.

"Mine too," said a third. "It's just dumb. Everybody knows snow runs in the Falls are the best."

"If you say so," said Tinker. "I prefer my spot here by the fire." He wrapped his arm around Bellamy to illustrate his point. The wolves whistled and howled teasingly. Bellamy's blush was adorable.

"I hear you're not a prince anymore," said the first were.

"What happened?" asked the second. "Couldn't cut it?"

Tinker smiled at the boys' ribbing. The jabs and jokes didn't sting like they might have only six months ago. Tinker had been on an amazing adventure and had done amazing things, and he'd come out the other side with a different perspective. These jokers—his *friends*—were completely harmless. Beneath their massive strength and claws and teeth, they were messed-up teenagers, just like him.

"You are right," said Quin. "Tinker is no longer the Goblin Prince. I am. Be sure to get that straight."

The wolf-shifters oohed and bowed comically to Quin.

"So what does that make you then?" the third were asked Tinker. "First place loser?"

Tinker opened his mouth to explain his exhaustive role as ambassador to Goblin City, but Hubble jumped in to answer instead.

"King," said Hubble.

"What?" asked the weres.

"While Tinker was in Goblin City, he was king," explained Hubble. "Once a king, retired or not, always king. That's just how it works."

"Oh, snap," said Natalie.

Tinker shrugged. "He *is* right." Sure, he'd been king for all of five seconds. He had never fully wielded the magic that was rightfully Quin's. And now, without the crown, he was as human as Natalie. An ever-so-slightly green-tinted human.

But the rest of Harmswood didn't need to know all the details.

The wolves all patted him on the back. "Way to go, man!"

"Congratulations!"

"Good to have you back, Tink. See you around."

"Yeah, see you!" Tinker called after them.

"Well, how about that." Bellamy slid down into Tinker's lap and put her arms around his neck. "My boyfriend is a king."

"Ambassador-Boyfriend King," said Tinker. "Or would it be King Ambassador-Boyfriend?"

Bellamy smiled. "We'll figure it out."

Honestly, it didn't matter what she called him. That smile

of Bellamy's made him feel a hundred feet tall. He was back at Harmswood where he belonged, surrounded by friends and love, with a bright future ahead for him and Goblin City alike.

It was the best day ever.

WANT TO KNOW MORE ABOUT SAM AND NATALIE?

The characters of Sam and Natalie originally appeared in a short story of mine called "The Were Four."

"The Were Four" was written specifically for an anthology about were-beings. I had a great premise: Four super-lame teen were-boys have a terrible band, and they want to compete in a local Battle of the Bands. I even polled a panel audience at DragonCon that year and chose from the worst were-forms they could come up with: a platypus, a mosquito, a sloth, and a piranha.

I wrote frantically, down to the wire to hit the deadline for submissions. I giggled as I hit Send on the email. My story was different and hilarious and awkward and EPIC.

And then I did the thing they tell you not to do: I read the comments. Buried beneath the submission guidelines, the editor said she was looking for "particularly dark stories."

Yeah. That would have been helpful to see *in the actual guidelines*.

"The Were Four" was pretty much the opposite of "particularly dark." The editor politely declined publication. I tried several other venues, but no dice. I was devastated that my fabulous little story wouldn't see the light of day.

Eventually, I published enough short stories to create a collection: *Wild & Wishful, Dark & Dreaming.* In that book I included three stories that were never able to find a home. "The Were Four" was one of those stories.

Fast forward to 2017.

When I was writing the D&D coffee shop scene in Chapter Two, I knew I needed more players than just Tinker and Hubble. It wasn't more than a heartbeat before Sam and Natalie sat down at that table, like they'd been there the whole time.

I also made "The Were Four" available as a stand-alone story, for those who are simply more curious about Sam and Natalie. I may have loved them before, but I *really* love them now. I hope you do too!

Please let me know what you think!

xox

~Alethea

ACKNOWLEDGMENTS

As always, a million thanks to Kristen Painter, a fantastic woman who created an even more fantastic world. Bless you for letting me play on your playground.

Venti thanks to Port St. Java, local coffee haunt and writing hangout for a few of us Rocket Girls here on the Space Coast. Here's to a great future of words written and caffeine consumed on comfy couches! (And if you borrowed this book from the Local Author shelf, please do us all a favor and put it back when you're done...)

Huge hugs to Keri Knutson, Kat Tipton, and Miya Jones, the team of goddesses who make sure my books and I are in the best shape possible!

And to Casey, my Bellamy, whom I fell in love with at the ripe old age of eleven. Best friend and Obi-Wan Kenobi, Princess to my Queen of Thieves, and partner on countless adventures—the ones that included dice and the ones that included a stage.

It was Casey who taught me to be an optimist. To see beyond the false walls made by clubs and cliques and create my own tribe. Even now, after so many years, she sees the best inside of me and inspires me to create magic.

May our friendship live on forever in these pages, and the thousands more to come.

Want your very own
Hallowed Bean
merchandise?
Visit Kristen Painter's
official Nocturne Falls
Swag Shop!

zazzle.com/kristenpainter1

ABOUT THE AUTHOR

New York Times and *USA Today* bestselling author Alethea Kontis is a princess, a fairy godmother, and a geek. She's known for screwing up the alphabet, making horror movies with her friends, narrating the occasional story, and ranting about fairy tales on YouTube.

Alethea's published works include novels, novellas, and companions in the universes of Arilland, Nocturne Falls, Barefoot Bay, and Sherrilyn Kenyon's Dark-Hunters. She is also responsible for the AlphaOops picture books; *Haven, Kansas; Wild & Wishful, Dark & Dreaming*; *The Wonderland Alphabet;* and *Diary of a Mad Scientist Garden Gnome*. Her short fiction, essays, and poetry have appeared in over fifty anthologies and magazines.

Alethea's YA fairy tale novel, *Enchanted*, won both the Gelett Burgess Children's Book Award and Garden State Teen Book Award. *Enchanted* was nominated for the Audie Award in 2013 and was selected for World Book Night in 2014. Both *Enchanted* and its sequel, *Hero*, were nominated for the Andre Norton Award. *Tales of Arilland*, a short story collection set in the same fairy tale world, won a second Gelett Burgess Award in 2015. The second book in The Trix Adventures, *Trix and the Faerie Queen*, was a finalist for the Dragon Award in 2016.

Princess Alethea was given the honor of speaking about fairy tales at the Library of Congress in 2013. In 2015, she gave a keynote address at the Lewis Carroll Society's Alice150 Conference in New York City, celebrating the 150th anniversary of *Alice's Adventures in Wonderland*. She also enjoys speaking at schools and festivals all over the US. (If forced to choose between all these things, she says middle schools are her favorite!)

Born in Burlington, Vermont, Alethea currently lives and writes on the Space Coast of Florida. She makes the best baklava you've ever tasted and sleeps with a teddy bear named Charlie. Find out more about Princess Alethea and the magic, wonderful world in which she lives here: https://www.patreon.com/princessalethea

∾

Want to know when Alethea has a new book out? Sign up for the newsletter! http://eepurl.com/YSmS1

∾

Connect with Princess Alethea Online!
www.aletheakontis.com
akontis@gmail.com
Facebook: Alethea Kontis
Twitter: @aletheakontis

ALSO BY ALETHEA KONTIS

The Truth About Cats and Wolves

Haven, Kansas

Fish Out of Water

Wild & Wishful, Dark & Dreaming

Diary of a Mad Scientist Garden Gnome

Tales of Arilland

Enchanted

Hero

Dearest / Messenger

Trixter

Trix and the Faerie Queen

AlphaOops: The Day Z Went First

AlphaOops: H is for Halloween

The Wonderland Alphabet

Beauty & Dynamite

The Dark-Hunter Companion (w/Sherrilyn Kenyon)

The Simi's ABCs (w/Sherrilyn Kenyon)

Want to know more about the Wonderful World of Princess
Alethea? Get info about new releases and sales, original essays,
Princess Alethea merchandise, and videos!

FOLLOW Alethea on Patreon!

Patreon.com/princessalethea

Made in the USA
San Bernardino, CA
26 December 2017